The Boss Man's Daughters 5

Lock Down Publications and
Ca$h Presents
The Boss Man's Daughters 5
A Novel by Aryanna

Lock Down Publications
P.O. Box 870494
Mesquite, Tx 75187

Visit our website
www.lockdownpublications.com

Copyright 2018 by The Boss Man's Daughter 5 Aryanna

First Edition September 2018
Printed in the United States of America

Lock Down Publications
Like our page on Facebook: Lock Down Publications @
www.facebook.com/lockdownpublications.ldp
Cover design and layout by: **Dynasty Cover Me**
Book interior design by: **Shawn Walker**
Edited by: **Jill Alicea**

Stay Connected with Us!

Text **LOCKDOWN** to 22828 to stay up-to-date with new releases, sneak peeks, contests and more…

Submission Guideline.

Submit the first three chapters of your completed manuscript to ldpsubmissions@gmail.com, subject line: Your book's title. The manuscript must be in a .doc file and sent as an attachment. The document should be in Times New Roman, double-spaced and in size 12 font. Also, provide your synopsis and full contact information. If sending multiple submissions, they must each be in a separate email.

Have a story but no way to send it electronically? You can still submit to LDP/Ca$h Presents. Send in the first three chapters, written or typed, of your completed manuscript to:

LDP: Submissions Dept
Po Box 870494
Mesquite, Tx 75187

DO NOT send original manuscript. Must be a duplicate.

Provide your synopsis and a cover letter containing your full contact information.

Thanks for considering LDP and Ca$h Presents.

Dedication

This book is dedicated to princess Natalie for her birthday. Happy Birthday, sweetheart, I love you!!!!!

Acknowledgments

I give all the Glory to God, first, because without him nothing would be possible. Thank you, Jesus, for helping me find my blessing in the struggle. I would like to thank my best friend, life partner, and soulmate, my Uno Nuno! I appreciate everything you've done and continue to do, but more than that, I appreciate the way you've fought for our relationship. I ain't made it easy, but hopefully, in the end, I make it worth it. I would like to thank my friends and family for continued support and love every day.

I especially have to thank Connor James for making me smile when I don't want to. Just remember, I'm gonna turn Natalie loose on you when you don't act right—Lol! I have to thank Mariah Grace and Jada Boo for the unconditional love you've always given me. You two are priceless.

I have to thank Big Byrd for ev-er-ything! I love you, enough said. My books may get old, but your love never does, and I'm so appreciative of it all. I have to thank my Lockdown family for the love and support, and Cash because it was still you who took a chance on me, first. Respect. I gotta shout out General Monk because his time has come. I see you, my dude! I also gotta shout out that PANDA, PANDA, PANDA! The love is real, and your dreams will be a reality.

Lastly, I wanna shout out them HATERS! Sorry, I don't have much ink for you these days, but I still appreciate the contributions you make to my motivational level. Now watch me level up! To all the real goons and goblins stuck behind the G-wall, I salute you. Keep your head up and only down to pray. With a heart full of love for the first time in a long time, I have to thank my namesake, Aryanna. I started this because of you so that you would know, I love you even when I'm too far away for you to hear my voice. Now you know the truth and I pray that comforts you forever, I love you baby!

Aryanna

Chapter 1
~Royal~
Nigeria

18 Months Later
November 2019

"It's so beautiful, and peaceful out here. It doesn't matter if it's sunrise or sunset, on any given day the beauty is breathtaking, and something everyone should experience before they die. Don't you agree? I gotta admit, I thought I knew a lot about, Africa and its rich history. But, there was nothing ever written in any book that can describe what you'll feel once you're here. It's like finding a piece of you, you had no idea, you'd lost. Does that make sense?

Well, maybe it doesn't to you, considering your journey to the motherland caused you to lose more than you'd planned. If I apologized for that, would it make you feel better? Probably not, because it's obvious I wouldn't sincerely mean it. Are any of you sorry?" I asked, pulling my gaze away from the hypnotizing view of the sunset in front of me, and turning it on the five men a few feet away.

The expressions on their faces didn't seem particularly contrite or remorseful, but it definitely lacked the smug arrogance they once sported.

"I won't lie and pretend being apologetic will change the situation you're in, but a little honesty at this point could go a long way. So, I'll ask you again, who sent you all to kill me?"

I didn't really export an answer from any of the men, not just because they'd been sufficiently tortured already without breaking, but because it was obvious whoever thought to send mercenaries would think to cover their tracks. It wasn't terribly important to know exactly which one of my beloved sisters had sent assassins to kill me but knowing would tell me, who I should kill first. This wasn't the first attempt made to get my brother and nephew back since I'd rescued them from their poor excuses of mothers a year and a half ago, but it *was* the first time they'd tried to kill me. I could smell their deportation from here, but that didn't make me regret my decision or feel sorry for them. It actually made me think, they still hadn't learned their lesson, so maybe they hadn't felt enough pain. I hopped down off the hood of my Land Rover and began pacing back and forth in front of the men who'd tried to take my life.

"Don't everyone speak at once. I'm pretty sure each of you knows how this movie ends. So, the only question is how do you want to die?" I asked, pulling my Glock .45 from the waist of my pants.

Not a single expression changed at the sight of my gun, but the sudden howling of a wild animal got their attention. It was clear each man was finally beginning to understand, that when you were buried up to your neck in the African desert, at night, there are a lot of ways to die. None of them painless or easy.

"I'm sure all of you know how powerful an animal's nose is so the blood you're covered in is probably already attracting a lot of attention. That beautiful sunset you see over my shoulder will be disappearing in a matter of minutes. But, whoever tells me what I want to know first won't find out what happens after dark. So, who sent you?" I asked, chambering a bullet into my gun.

Three of the men's faces remained blank, but the other two men couldn't keep their eyes from darting around or keep out the fear flooding them.

"Sir, if you want me to put cameras on each man, the time has come, because we must be leaving soon," Colonel Fazi said, coming to stand beside me.

I nodded my head in approval, and the short fat man immediately got to work fitting a body cam on the little clothing that was still attached to each man. As badly as I wanted to watch the show in person, I didn't want to become a side dish to the main course, so watching it from afar would have to do. With each passing second, I could tell reality was setting in for the two men who kept trying to peek into the approaching night, so I stood in front of them and waited. I had no doubts each man had taken this assignment because it sounded easy, almost too good to be true since all that was required was killing a thirteen-year-old kid and rescuing two toddlers.

It was a guarantee that at this moment, every man understood they'd been lied to. Eighteen months ago, I wasn't a typical eleven-year-old, mainly because of how my mother raised me, and later because of how my sisters' lifestyle influenced me. I saw too much, which meant, I knew even more, so when it was time to make my play no one saw it coming. I was in their blind spot. After having miscalculated so badly, I would've thought my sisters would've learned not to underestimate me, but it seemed I was wrong. These men would pay for it, though.

"Last chance," I said, looking at the two men in front of me.

"Syndicate—it was a syndicate out of Chicago that offered the contract," The only white man in the group blurted.

"And what did they tell you?" I asked.

"Just that you'd kidnapped two young boys and you were hiding out in Africa. Told us where to find you, and that the local government could be bought."

"Well that is true, but they neglected to tell you, I'm a very wealthy young man, which means the government and military here are already in my pocket. The name of this syndicate?" I asked, curiously.

"I-I don't know the actual name, or the players involved, but a catering company named 'Everybody Eats' is their front."

Aryanna

Not surprising, I was familiar with the company, since it had contributed to financing the empire, I was currently growing. Now that I had the info I needed I could get on with the show.

"Good talk, you earned this," I said, pointing the gun at his face, pulling the trigger.

"Let's go," I said to the colonel, going back to my truck, climbing in the passenger seat.

Once Fazi was behind the wheel, he signaled for the SUV behind us to back up, and we followed their lead until we were a safe distance away so that we wouldn't spook the animals. I turned on my iPad and logged into the cameras live feed, which allowed me to see and hear everything the mercenaries could. At first, there was silence, not even talking amongst each other, but as the nightlife came alive, reality took its toll and farfetched escape plans began flying. It was entertaining, to say the least, making me wish, I'd brought some popcorn to go with the show.

For thirty minutes we sat there as the suspense built until finally, I saw the eyes of one of Africa's many predators glowing as it approached tonight's dinner. When one pair of eyes suddenly became three I hit the buttons necessary to record what was about to go down. The panic in the men's voices gave me chills in a way, I hadn't experienced since losing my virginity. Out of all the predators that could've made a meal out of them they were coming face to face with one of the worse. A pack of hyenas.

The animals were curious on approach, but that quickly changed when they realized their prey couldn't run from them. Suddenly, the night erupted into screams mixed with the sounds of flesh tearing, and bones being crushed by powerful jaws on a mission. I watched with awe and fascination as one man's lips disappeared in a quick bite, followed swiftly by his nose and a good portion of his jaw. Still, he screamed and begged for mercy from those incapable of giving it. For ten solid minutes, I watched completely trans-fixed.

Just when I thought it was over, it got more interesting. I could tell that a noise in the distance had spooked the hyenas because all of them stopped eating at once, their gaze and attention shifted towards something I couldn't see. I'd been in Africa long enough to know, the only thing that stopped a predator from finishing a meal was the threat of something bigger making a meal out of them. Sure enough, a fast-moving female lion came racing out of the shadows, followed by four equally graceful big female cats, causing the hyenas to scatter like project roaches.

After that the feeding frenzy took a turn, because one lion took a man's head completely off in a single bite, prompting the others to do the same. Then they got to work using their huge paws to dig the bodies out of the ground, and before I knew it dinner had become take out.

"I love Africa," I whispered, smiling.

"There is no place like it. Shall we go?" Fazi asked.

"Yeah, we can go home now."

I continued watching the live feed until every camera was destroyed, then I watched it again to make sure all the good parts were recorded. Now that, I'd eliminated the im-mediate threat of those trying to kill me, it was time to focus on the bringer of this particular rain storm. I'd spared their lives, and provided a safe, sane, upbringing for my brother and nephew, but still, my warning about interfering with us wasn't heeded. Did that mean, it was now okay for me to kill everyone, I'd left behind?

I wouldn't lose any sleep over Bone, Lil Boy, or Big Baby but how would I feel about taking the lives of Free, Angel, Destiny, and Kamile? It was obvious at this point, they didn't give a fuck about *my* life. The reason I'd taken B.J. and Prince was to do shit differently than they had. Somehow, I was now asking myself if I was actually better than they were.

Aryanna

"Fazi, I know who sent those men," I confessed.

"I figured you did, considering your list of enemies outside of this country could not be that long."

"You know I'm not the type to make enemies Fazi. The only reason, I've had to since coming to Africa is to prove I was not to be fucked with or treated like a child," I replied.

"A message you sent loud and clear. What message do you intend to send to those enemies in the United States of America?"

"That's what I'm asking myself because these aren't normal enemies. They're family, and they're formidable."

"I take it this has something to do with what brought you here in the first place," Fazi replied, gravely.

Fazi was one of the very few people who knew the exact circumstances that had brought me to my current spot in life. To most, there was a lot of mystery about the man-child who had a lot of money, two children, and no tolerance for any sideways bullshit. Fazi had been the first man I'd sat down with because once upon a time he'd been Daphney's husband. Our relationship had been built upon my gift of Daphney to him because he'd viewed her desertion as an ultimate betrayal, therefore making me the giver of long-awaited revenge.

Some would've viewed my move as callow, but to me, it was simply strategy because I knew I couldn't trust her, so I couldn't keep her around. Plus, having an Allie within the army allowed me to establish myself, and become entrenched in the corruption out here. I wasn't foolish enough to trust Fazi but I knew he was loyal to money, so I trusted him not to cut off his nose to spite his face.

"Yes, this has everything to do with what brought me here," I replied.

"You and the children are safe here. The mercenaries never had a chance of getting to you or them. That will always be the case as long as I am alive. What is it that worries you?"

"Their desperation has me slightly concerned, and it's making me consider being proactive against their attacks," I replied, honestly.

"I know good men who will take the job all you have to do is give the word."

I contemplated his words while preparing to send the file containing tonight's festivities to the person directly responsible.

"I'll give them one more chance but be ready because two warnings is one too many."

Aryanna

Chapter 2
~Free~
Brazil

The bounty of the orange blood off the blue water signaling a new day approaching would've brought serenity and contentment to most, but not me. For me, sunrise brought pain because somewhere in this world my son was without his mother, and it brought me barely containable rage for the same reason. Times passage didn't lessen either feeling in me, because the wound of having B.J. taken from me was not one that would ever heal. For my daughter Grace's sake. I tried to be as normal as I could, but a year and a half later, it was still almost impossible to be anything other than borderline crazy with grief. Deep down, I knew B.J. wasn't dead because Royal loved him too much to do anything like that, but my heart still mourned every second my son wasn't with me. Today would be day number five hundred and forty-eight of continuous mourning, and just like all the others, I didn't know how I'd survive it with my sanity intact.

"Figured I'd find you out here, mind if I join you?"

"Suit yourself," I replied, not bothering to look at her.

"You know it's crazy how most people come to the beach to relax and look for a peace of mind, but we come just to look for answers. Or maybe even a way to turn back the hands of time."

Had it been anyone other than Kamile speaking to my pain, right now, I probably would've lost my shit, but the sad truth was no one understood better than she did. A woman I'd once fantasized about killing was now my sister wife in grief, because my brother had taken her son too, and almost her life in the process. Kamile's son Prince had been all she had left in the world as a testament to the love she'd shared with my father. Having him taken had pushed her down a dark hole of self-destruction.

My own pain blinded me to hers until I found her on this very beach with a gun in her mouth playing Russian roulette. That day changed the nature of our relationship more than any other, before it because by saving her from herself, I'd saved me. The guilt I'd felt from the moment, I'd read the letter Royal left explaining his actions made me want to put a bullet in my brain, too. It wasn't something I could admit to anyone, and if others felt it they probably assumed I'd kept going for my baby girl, but I hadn't. Seeing Kamile and saving Kamile was the only thing that had kept me from completely breaking, and now those days were behind me. I could only hope the same was true for her.

"You okay?" I asked, glancing at her before continuing to watch the sunrise in the distance.

"I think you know the answer to that question."

"And you know exactly what I'm asking," I replied, firmly.

"I guess I do. I'm fine sis, at least when it comes to whether or not, I wanna kill myself. I don't want to do that anymore. I want to kill him."

I didn't need to ask who *'him'* was because the ugly truth was, I'd had delicious thoughts about killing him too, brother or no brother. I know not even Father-God could've seen shit getting *this* sideways, but would he have given me permission to murder his son? That was just one of many questions that kept me up at night.

"You can't kill him Kamile, Father-God, wouldn't have—"

"With all due respect, Jonathan ain't here, and the baby *we* made has been kidnapped by the son he never knew. Do you think he would've allowed that?" she asked.

I wanted to say yes, he would've because he would've never chosen between his kids. But, this was a situation that had the potential to bring out the ruthless savage in any parent.

"We'll never know what he would've done, so all we can control is what *we* do. I'm not ready to live with taking Royal's life," I said, honesty.

"Not ready? Free, it's been a year and a half, and that's felt like *ten* years! Your son is two years old now and mine will be two in a few more months. We haven't seen them since they were *babies* Free, cute innocent *babies*. And you're not *ready*? I know you have a husband and a new baby, but Prince is *all* I have. I can't keep waiting for a child to decide my baby's future. I'm ready," she declared, passionately.

The emotion in her voice already had me looking at her, but I saw something in her eyes when she made her last statement, that made me pay closer attention.

"You're ready? What does that mean?" I asked, carefully.

I could see the determination clearly in her hazel eyes, but her lips weren't moving.

"Kamile, what does that *mean*?" I asked again.

"Nothing. I'm just tired of waiting for Royal to give me my son back."

"I completely understand that trust me, but what are we gonna do? The last rescue attempt only showed us how corrupt shit is in Africa, because not even the U.S Embassy over there would get our kids back," I replied, as frustrated as she was.

"I don't know what to do, but I'm damn sure not talking about going any legal route. Money is law over there, and we know all too well that Royal has money."

Thinking about how he drained all our accents still stung, almost as much as him taking my child. We'd spent our entire lives fighting to rise above the mud from which we were born, and in moments our own flesh and flood had tossed us back. If it hadn't been for Kamile's connections that allowed me to revive the street empire Bone and I had built from a distance, as well as her having money hidden that Royal *hadn't* found. We would've been fucked. We were nowhere near where we once were, which meant our arms weren't long enough to box with Royal from a money aspect. Kamile was making it clear she was thinking on another level anyway.

"Kamile, we're sharing and living the same pain and having Grace doesn't lessen mine, because she's a constant reminder of the brother she's growing up without. I can't put into *words* how badly I miss B.J., but I can't kill, Royal. I promised my dad, I'd save him."

"Well, I didn't make that promise," she replied, quickly.

As she turned her gaze to the horizon. I didn't know where this conversation was going, but it was giving me bad vibes.

"Kamile—"

The sudden chimes from her phone notification system interrupted my thoughts, but I could tell she was eager to avoid my full court press because she readily pulled her phone from her dress pocket. It almost looked like she'd been not so patiently waiting on something, especially considering how early in the morning it was, and if that was the case then the anger I saw creeping over her meant sad news.

"What is it?" I asked.

She didn't answer me right away, didn't even look in my direction, but instead continued to stare intently at her phone screen like she was hypnotized.

"What is it?" I repeated, becoming slightly worried.

She still didn't answer, but she did pass me her phone, before standing up and walking to the water's edge. I thought she was simply gonna walk in fully clothed, but she just stood there and let the water run over her feet. I turned my attention to her phone in my hand and saw a video waiting to be played with an option for audio. When I tapped the screen to see what it was, I was immediately overwhelmed by multiple voices talking at once. I couldn't make sense of the words or see anyone, but their fear was easy to decipher.

Through each passing moment, I could hear the panic level rising, but I didn't understand why because all I could see was growing darkness from every camera angle. Suddenly, the voices were no longer voices, they were screams I was entirely familiar with. They were the screams of death. I watched with eerie fascination, a killing, unlike anything I'd ever seen or done in my life and was helpless to turn away despite how gruesome it was. When the video ended I had to watch it again just to make sure, I didn't miss anything, and by the time the last camera went dark Kamile had made her way back to where I was sitting.

"What the fuck is this some type of new age snuff film? Who sent you this shit?" I asked.

"It's a long story," she replied, evasively.

"Why do I have a feeling that it's a story I need to hear?"

I could tell she was uncomfortable, and that was making me nervous.

"Start talking, Kamile," I demanded.

"You're not gonna like it"

"Yeah, I already figured that much out, by how shady you're being right now. So, spit it out already," I replied, with growing impatience.

"I know the men in that video."

"How do you know them, you couldn't even see their faces or bodies."

"I know them because I hired them. They were mercenaries," she replied slowly.

"Mercenaries why the fuck would you—"

Suddenly, I knew the answer to the question I no longer needed to ask, and everything she'd been saying made perfect sense.

"Y—you went after, Royal? Bitch are you *crazy!*" I yelled, swinging a wild right hook that just barely clipped her chin.

Aryanna

I was hoping the bitch would put her hands up, so I could lay hands on her, but she chose the smarter option and ran for the house screaming Bone's name. Of course, I took off behind her because not even my husband would save her from this ass whooping. I had to give her credit because she was quick on her feet, but I still caught her by a fist full of hair just as she was about to run from the porch into the living room.

"Free wait, I—"

I didn't let her finish that sentence before trying to shove my fist down her throat. My follow-up punch landed in her eye socket, with a beautiful smack that fueled my motivation, as my hand found its way around her throat, so I could hold her still.

"Free, what the fuck?" Destiny yelled, coming out of the house.

"Stay out of this," I growled, finding another spot on Kamile's face to plant my jab, and delivering swiftly.

Just as I was winding up for my next pitch, I felt familiar hands snatching me into the air like I weighed nothing at all.

"Bone put me down, I'ma *kill* this bitch!" I swore, trying in vain to get loose.

"Not until you tell me why, it's *too* early in the morning to kill a bitch for no reason," Bone replied, carrying me back out onto the beach.

"Put me *the fuck* down," I demanded, angrily.

"Tell me what's going on first, Freedom," Bone replied, patiently.

He was still walking with me thrown over his shoulder like he was a fireman when I spotted Kamile's phone in the sand.

"Put me down so I can show you on her phone," I replied, knowing I couldn't win this fight with him.

He did what I asked, then stood there with me watching the video.

"I don't understand," he said, after the conclusion of the video.

I quickly relayed the conversation Kamile and I had and the revelation that came out after I watched the video.

"Ohhhh," Bone said, slowly.

"Exactly, now will you please get out of my way, so I can finish beating the pretty off that bitch."

"No, but, I can go with you back to the house for a civilized conversation," he replied, taking my hand, leading me in the direction we'd come.

"Talk? Do you understand what she *did*? What the outcome could've been?"

"I do, but do you think she's in her right frame of mind, babe? You know what she's going through. I'm not making excuses for her at all, but we need to talk to her if for no other reason, then to prevent another attack on, Royal," he reasoned.

I'd sooner bite my tongue off than admit he was even the slightest bit right, so I kept my mouth shut until we got back to the house. I took pleasure in seeing Kamile sitting on a lounge chair with ice covering her left eye and blood still leaking from her busted lip. If I had my way she'd be getting some more action in the near future.

"Kamile, what were you thinking?" Bone asked, in a disappointing tone.

"I was thinking I haven't held or seen my son in eighteen months. I was thinking there's no way we grown ass adults are supposed to be at the mercy of some fucking kid! And yes, I was thinking if he had to die for my son to live, then so be it," she replied, hastily.

"Do you not see that your actions could've got your son *killed*? You hired *mercenaries* and them mufuckas ain't known for their search and rescue skills dummy," I replied, with equal hostility.

"They were paid to kill, Royal, and get *both* of our sons back, Free," Kamile replied, defensively.

23

"Well, we see how *that* turned out you simple minded—
"

"Wait, hold up Free, did you just say you tried to kill, Royal?" Destiny asked, looking at Kamile with a serious side eye.

"Yes, I did, I want my son back!" Kamile yelled, dissolving into hysterical tears.

Her wails of pain pierced my soul, forcing my anger to run and hide as my own pain bowed to hers. I felt what she felt, but somehow, I'd managed to fight off the separation I could see in her. Seeing her now told me that her actions were only the beginning because she'd rather kill or die than live without her son. I couldn't fault her because as a mother, I understood exactly how she felt. When I looked at Bone and Destiny I could see they understood, too. Something had to be done.

Chapter 3
~Angel~
Brazil

"Oh-shit-shit-fuck! Oh, ba-by," I moaned, riding Lil' Boy faster, as I felt the delirious fog of an orgasm clouding my brain.

"I'ma cum-cum with you," he promised, grabbing ahold of my ass cheeks just the way I liked, pulling me down on him with enough force to make me take all the dick he had.

Once upon a time, I'd feared that action because my nigga was hung long enough to make a force reconsider, but now I couldn't live until I felt him in my stomach.

"I'm-I'm-do it," I demanded, squeezing my eyes shut tight as the fog lifted and the most beautiful paradise was laid before me.

The moment I felt him push a finger into my asshole, I came all the way unglued, loving how all the colors of the rainbow were dancing on the back of my eyelids while my orgasm washed over me like liquid gold. Moments later, I felt his explosion and kept right on riding him like a woman possessed because his dick was good till the last drop. When I tried to move off top of him, he pulled me against his chest like always, and kissed me with a gentleness, no one outside of these four walls would ever expect him to demonstrate. My future husband was the definition of the word goon and goblin all rolled into one, but with me, he was the sweetest, most loving man, I'd ever been with, and I appreciated the versatility.

"Good morning," I said, kissing him again.

"*Great* morning," he countered, wrapping me up in his long arms.

I loved that I never had to ask him to hold me, it was just something he loved to do because he understood it made me feel safe. Having your man as your best friend was too important to be understated, so I made sure to show my appreciation in every way I could as much as possible.

"What do you want for breakfast?" I asked.

"How about a little more of you."

"You think you can handle all that?" I asked, seductively.

"You still feel me throbbing inside you like a heartbeat, don't you? I'm good for another round."

"Let's see how long you last," I challenged, kissing along his jawline and down his neck, then further down to his chest.

By the time, I reached the last AB in his six pack I could feel the tension that had built in his body just from a few well-placed kisses, and innocent licks. In the last year and a half, we'd learned a lot about each other, including the fact that I had no gag reflex. He may have been talking tough a second ago, but we both knew he didn't stand a chance.

"That's not f-fair," he whimpered, as soon as I had his dick in both of my hands, kissing the head of it like we'd just met.

I wrapped my lips around him gently and savored the flavors of our lovemaking on my tongue while sucking him like a tootsie pop. I knew exactly how many licks it took to get to his center, and after teasing him by only sucking on the head, I pulled back, so I could lick slowly from the base of his shaft to the tip again.

"Fuck!" He yelled, trying in vain to keep his back on the mattress.

"Surrender," I demanded, before traveling the same path I'd just taken two more times, even slower.

When I finally got around to devouring his dick an inch at a time until there was nothing left, I could feel his entire body shaking like he was experiencing withdrawals. His dick was too big for this to be a fast adventure, so I took my time, bobbing up and down at a snail's pace while gently caressing his balls in my hand.

"Angel!" he cried, breathlessly.

I knew from past experiences he was fighting not to make the mistake of grabbing my hand because the only time he'd ever done that it almost cost him two to three inches. I could already feel the trembling that started in his toes and spread upward, signaling he was just about to lose the battle *and* war. I pulled my head back until I only had half of him in my mouth while using my other hand to squeeze the base of his shaft, as I moved it up and down swiftly. His strangled screams rolled through our condo just as his hot, salty, cum erupted in my mouth. The sight of him lying there, weaker than a newborn, left a satisfied smile on my face because it had taken me a while to own this part of my sexuality. I wasn't a virgin anymore, I was a certified snake charmer.

"I guess I'll cook breakfast now, and you can try to find the brain cells you just lost," I said, getting out of bed.

"I'll get you—get you back," he threatened, in a hoarse whisper.

I laughed in victory as I left our bedroom and stopped in our son's room to check on him. The only thing I loved more than being the soulmate to Lil' Boy was being a mother to our son, God Angel Walker. He was literally everything I never knew, I wanted, and every day I opted to wake up and be his mom was a true blessing for me. It was also a day, I got to empathize with Free and Kamile because I didn't know how I'd ever survive if I lost him. I'd found a way to be at peace with losing my dad with Lil' Boy's help, but to lose my son would be too much.

I expected to find him sleeping, but instead he was sitting up in his bed playing with his toys and carrying on a full-blown conversation with himself. Catching him in precious moments like this only added to the vault of memories that would be mine and his to share forever. So, I just stood there quietly and watched. I don't know how long I stayed frozen in that spot, drinking in my son's innocent bounty, but eventually, I felt Lil' Boy's presence behind me. When I turned to look at him, I'd expected to find the same smile of joy I was wearing, but the look in his eyes said there was a problem.

He took my hand and led me back to the bedroom, closing the door behind us.

"What's wrong?" I asked immediately.

"I just got a text from my brother saying we need to come to the house for a family meeting."

"That still doesn't answer the question of what's wrong. So, tell me what we're walking into, because I know Big Baby told you," I replied, feeling my morning glow fading fast.

Lil' Boy's hesitation was a clear indication that bad news was soon to flow from his mouth.

"Apparently, Kamile made a move against, Royal."

"What kind of move?" I asked, slowly, already not liking where this was going.

"A bad move. She hired mercenaries to kill him and bring the young ones back to the states."

"I'm guessing that didn't go so well with my sisters," I replied, going to the dresser and pulling out clothes to throw on.

If Destiny and Free hadn't taken Kamile's head off yet, it was only a matter of time, which meant we had to get over there quickly.

"I don't know how bad shit got, but Big Baby wants us over there, a.s.a.p," he replied.

"I bet he does. I know Royal did some fucked up shit, but he's still alive because of the promise Free made to our dad. She's not gonna go back on that, and Kamile has probably come to that realization, which is why she's gone rogue. I may not know exactly what happened, but if Kamile tries that shit again, Free *will* kill her."

"We better get over there then," he said, reaching for his own clothes.

After pulling on a t-shirt and some shorts I went back to God's room to get him dressed.

"Hey, little man, you wanna go see your aunties and your cousins?"

"Yeah!" He screamed, excitedly, jumping up out of bed and running towards me.

I scooped him into my arms and covered his face with kisses until he was laughing hysterically. He was big to be only fourteen months old, which meant the days of me holding him high above my head were fleeting, and even more precious. I wanted to savor this moment, but it was a half hour drive from where we lived to the house everybody else shared, so we had to get on the move. It was times like this when I really regretted our decision to move out, but it was just too crowded now that we all had kids. I quickly put some clothes on God. Ten minutes later we were all in the Range Rover headed for the beach.

I adjusted the speakers, so the music would play exclusively in the back of the truck, so we could talk without God overhearing. He may have been a little kid incapable of understanding what we were talking about, but from the moment I'd found out I was pregnant, I swore to protect his innocence at all costs.

"When did all of this happen?" I asked.

"I don't know, all I know is shit hit the fan sometime this morning."

"I wanna be mad with Kamile, but I honestly don't know what I would do in her situation," I said, looking back lovingly at our son.

He looked more and more like Lil' Boy every day, proving that the DNA test, I'd had done right after his birth had been unnecessary.

"You wouldn't have to do anything in that situation. I'd handle it."

Aryanna

The determination in his voice made his meaning clear, and honestly, I couldn't expect anything less than all-out war if *anyone* tried to take his son or hurt me. He'd proven a long time ago what was important to him, and that there was *nothing* he wouldn't do to protect that. I loved Royal even though, he'd done the unthinkable, because I still remembered the sweet little boy I'd picked up from boarding school! I hadn't regained all the memories I'd lost, but I had more of my life back now then I had after waking up from my coma. Looking back, I could see that I'd assumed Royal would stay that innocent kid, naïve to the world that existed around him, but that was naïve on my part.

He'd been too smart to stay dumb, and none of us saw it, *I* didn't see it! I carried a certain amount of guilt for that. At the same time, I felt for Kamile, so it was my hope that I could talk her off the ledge she was standing on. The rest of the ride was spent with me trying to figure out how to bring a peaceful end to this standoff with Royal but I kept coming up empty because I had no idea where my little brothers head was at.

"You ready?" I asked once Lil' Boy brought the truck to a stop in the driveway.

"Yeah. I'll get God, while you go find out what's going on."

"Oh sure, you take the easy job," I replied, shaking my head as I climbed out of the truck and made my way towards the house.

Normally, I would hear Faith and Grace playing as soon as I crossed the threshold, but there was an eerie silence when I came through the front door. I made my way through the house and out onto the porch, where I found everybody. The first thing I noticed was that Kamile's eye was swollen shut, and her bottom lip was the same size as her forearm.

"Damn, I see what you had for breakfast," I said, wincing slightly.

"Real funny bitch," Kamile replied, sullenly.

Looking around at those I considered family, I saw that everyone was wearing the same serious expression, which meant now wasn't the time to be cracking jokes.

"Where are the kids?" Lil' Boy asked, joining us on the porch with God in his arms.

"Playing in my bedroom," Free replied.

Lil' Boy disappeared in that direction.

"A'ight, so what the fuck is going on?" I asked.

Destiny passed me a cell phone, and I could see a video waiting to be played, but nobody said anything. I tapped the screen to view it, and it only took a few minutes for me to understand why nobody was talking.

"Oh shit," I said softly.

"That's one way to sum it up," Destiny replied.

"What is this?" I asked.

"That's what happened to the mercenaries, Kamile sent at, Royal," Free replied, clearly still pissed off.

"Royal, orchestrated this? I can't believe that," I said, genuinely, shocked.

"Believe it," Kamile said, sourly.

As I was trying to wrap my head around what was going on Lil' Boy reappeared at my side, and I passed him the cell-phone.

"Oh shit," he said, after watching it twice.

"Exactly," I replied.

"So, the conclusion we've come to is that something has to be done," Free said.

"Something like what?" I asked, cautiously.

"I'm not breaking my promise to dad," Free replied, firmly.

"Unfortunately," Kamile mumbled.

"Bitch—" Free said, in warning.

"Stay focused," Bone interjected.

"Okay. The bottom line is we've gotta put an end to this shit before things are done that can't be undone. We've managed to come up with somewhat of a plan, but it's completely unorthodox for us," Destiny admitted.

"Well, now I'm sufficiently curious," I replied, wondering what type of fuckery we were about to get into.

"Before we get to that I need to say something," Kamile said.

All eyes turned to her expectantly.

"I know none of you agree with the decision I made to go after, Royal. I know you wouldn't before I did it. For that reason, I can't offer a sincere apology. What I can say is that I won't break your trust again, even if this newly hatched plan doesn't work out. I know I haven't really been myself since-since my son was taken, but at one point in time, I prided myself on keeping shit one hundred. I need to get back to that. So, no more sneaky shit," she concluded.

I didn't know whether everyone else believed her or not, but I did.

"Don't make me kick your ass again," Free warned.

"See, I *knew* that looked like your handy work," I said, hoping to ease the tension.

My comment at least made Destiny chuckle.

"Back to the business at hand," Bone said.

"So, what's the plan?" I asked.

"Well, we know Royal, is hiding behind our money in Africa, and it's evident he's been smart enough to put it to good use if he can make light work out of five trained killers. We also know that as long as he has money nobody in that country will turn on him, so we have to make his money useless," Free said.

"And how do we do that, I mean he stole almost a quarter of a billion, which he's undoubtedly been growing. He ain't stupid, we've seen his I.Q. scores to verify that," I replied.

"No, he ain't stupid, and you're right he's definitely been growing the money. We make it useless by making him an enemy of the state," Free said.

"An enemy of *what* state?" I asked, confused as to where she was going with this.

"The United States of America, of course."

Aryanna

Chapter 4
~Destiny~
Six Days Later

"I'm still not liking this idea, I think we should try to get the info we need some other way," I said.

The look Big Baby gave me was easy to decipher, especially considering the repeated text he'd sent telling me this was the best way. I respected that he wanted to be our eyes and ears on the ground in Africa, but the truth was he was needed here more. When Black Sam was murdered it was Big Baby who stayed with me during my darkest hours. It was him who helped me the most with my daughter, because even though she wasn't biologically mine, every time I looked at her I saw me, Sam, and the future we'd wanted.

In the aftermath, of her death, it had been almost impossible to look at Faith, but Big Baby made sure to keep her around me. The love of my sisters was something I'd relied on my entire life, but it was the love he'd given me that saved me, and I was terrified to lose that.

"Royal knows what you look like, and you know he's gotta have eyes everywhere after, Kamile's failed attempt on him," I stated, logically.

Big Baby immediately went to his phone and fired a text at me. The text said, that he didn't plan to walk up to Royal's front door and ring the bell like the Avon lady.

"I know you're not just gonna walk up to the front door and ring the bell smartass, but your ass is too big to be invisible," I replied, frustrated by the smile he was giving me.

I thought he wasn't taking this situation seriously, but his next text proved me wrong. He wanted to know what had me so worried when he'd done way more dangerous shit for the family before. For a moment, all I could do was look at him, wondering how I could put what I felt into words, that wouldn't ruin the best friendship I'd ever had outside of my sisters. As crazy as it would probably sound to anyone except me and Big Baby, our friendship was deeper than even mine had been with Black Sam.

He and I had *years* of dirt under our fingernails, and those same hands were covered in blood. The bond that had formed couldn't be defined by words, and I'd already lost too much to lose that, too.

"Daddy, I made this," Faith said, coming into my room, handing Big Baby a picture.

I'd taken Faith from Monster when she was only six months old so the only father she knew was Big Baby and she loved him unconditionally. He loved her just the same and worshipped the ground that his two-year-old princess walked on. He didn't take the picture she offered, but instead pulled her onto his lap and gave her hugs and kisses until she squealed in delight. My heart always melted when I watched them together, not only because of how cute they were but because it reminded me of how much my daddy had loved me.

Being a father could warm even the coldest of men, and a little girl's bond with her dad was more than sacred. As badly as I'd wanted to murder Royal for what he'd done to Black Sam, the love and respect, I still had for my dad stopped me. I prayed that Big Baby and Faith would always have that type of bond.

"Where's my picture, Faith Walker?" I asked, screwing my face up like I was hurt.

The '*oh shit*' look she turned on me was priceless and had me and Big Baby laughing until tears were in our eyes.

"I make it mommy," she said, scooting down off Big Baby's lap, making a mad dash from the room.

When she was gone Big Baby held up the picture of three stick figures that undoubtedly represented me, him, and her.

"That's part of the reason, I don't want you on the front-line. For this, Faith would be devastated if something happened to you, so would I," I confessed.

The look he gave me was two parts understanding one-part confusion, which made it clear, I was gonna have to spell it all the way out for him. After getting up and closing the door, I sat on the side of my bed closest to him, so we could have this come to Jesus.

"It's obvious you need to hear the words, so the real problem is that I'm scared of losing you. I've been through too fucking much to have to go through that, too, so I think someone else should do recon on Royal in Africa. There, I said it."

Following my declaration, I couldn't tell if he was blinking slowly because he was fucking with me, or because he didn't believe what I'd just told him. After some suspenseful seconds, he shot me another text.

"Don't you know that I'd always make it back to you two?" I read aloud.

"We've both been in this game long enough to know that's not something you can promise," I said, truthfully.

His next message came in all capital letters, telling me he *was* making that promise though, and I should trust him.

"You *know* I trust you, nigga, you're my best friend! I just can't lose you, and you've already seen that Royal, is on that bullshit," I replied.

We shared a moment of silent communication and I could see some indecision on his face, but then he put his fingers back to work with lightning speed. I could read the frustration in the bunching of his eyebrows. I had a feeling I knew why, but once I actually started reading his text, I realized I'd been *way* off.

"Since we were teenagers I've rode for you and with you, right or wrong, good, bad, and ugly. I didn't do it because I had to, or even because I wanted to, but because of the love and loyalty, I have for you. I love Free, and Angel, but I've always loved you more," I read softly.

After reading that I just kept staring at my phone screen, overcome by emotion and memories of all the shit we'd been through over the years. I couldn't count a time when he hadn't been there, even when I'd tried to push him away. He never judged me for my bullshit, he simply laced up his boots and waded into it with me. Knowing all of this, and even having my memories as tangible proof, still couldn't force me to believe the promise he'd made to come back to me and Faith.

"Big Baby you can't—"

Suddenly my argument was silenced by the fact, that he'd closed the short distance between us, and his lips were now on mine. My first reaction was to freeze as the voice in my head screamed '*oh shit*', but I quickly recovered and did something unintended. I let myself fall. Not just backward on the bed, as I welcomed his weight on top of me, but I let myself lower the protective shield I'd worn around my heart since losing my woman. I opened the door to the emotion he was bringing me, and let myself fall because I knew he'd be there to catch me. The passion of his kiss clouded my brain so fast, I didn't realize he had me naked from the waist down until his fingers waved hello to my pussy lips.

His touch was soft, yet firm, and within seconds my whole body was singing in appreciation as demonstrated by the increased wetness coating his fingers, and the moans I was fighting not to let loose. For the first time in our relationship we both were communicating without words, and without there being any risks of a misunderstanding. When he pulled his fingers out of me, the seconds until he was in between my legs ready to give me what I wanted were torturous, but his first stroke let me know it was worth the wait.

"Slow," I moaned softly, already feeling that big dick ran in the family, and knowing that, slow and steady was the only way to take it.

I hadn't had a man inside me in so long that for a second, I knew real fear, but the look of love in Big Baby's eyes pushed my fear to the side. He took his time, going a little deeper with each stroke until my pussy welcomed him home with a loving hug that told him it was okay to take it to the next level. I wanted to lock my legs around his waist, but before I could he spread them wide as he put increasing power into his blows. The love still shined bright in his eyes, but so did the hunger. I'd never just let anyone, man, or woman, fuck me without me giving it right back to them, but this good dick had me seeing stars and clutching my sheets tight enough to make my hands cramp.

"Don't-don't stop," I begged, completely unashamed by my submission.

Faster and harder he dove into me until his blows created a hurricane that forced me to put my own hands over my mouth to keep the entire house from knowing what was going on. Even though I'd stopped screams, the sounds from our lovemaking were still getting louder because he had my pussy gushing, making the satisfying slap of our bodies colliding echo off the walls. I fought against the tremors still rocking my body, pulled him close, and rolled him onto his back without taking the dick out of me.

"My turn," I whispered, leaning down to lay claim to his juicy lips while moving my hips in slow circles.

I could feel his heart already thundering in his chest, but it kicked up a notch when I began bouncing straight up and down on him. Every time I hit the bottom of his dick it knocked the wind out of me, but with breathless determination, I rode him faster still.

"Mommy picture!" Faith yelled, knocking on the bedroom door.

The look in his eyes was begging me not to stop, and the look I gave him told him, I couldn't even if I wanted to, so onward I rode. I could feel his dick pounding harder inside of me with each passing second, forcing me to sit straight up on it and take us home.

"Mommy, daddy, picture!" Faith yelled, banging on the door now.

"Wait-just-just wait, baby!" I yelled back.

The look of shock and awe on his face told me what was coming right before I felt his body shudder and release into me. Two strokes later, I joined him, unable to silence my moans of ecstasy as I found what existed beyond heaven.

"Destiny, why you got this baby out here hollering, you know—ohhhhkay," Free said, from the doorway.

I turned just in time to see Free keeping Faith from seeing what was going on in the room and quickly shutting the door on us. When I looked at Big Baby the horrified expression on his face made me laugh, especially because I didn't know if it was because Faith had *almost* caught us, or because Free had *actually* caught us.

"It's okay," I said, kissing him again while still trying to wrap my mind around what had just happened.

When I'd woke up this morning I damn sure hadn't seen this coming. Now I didn't know what was supposed to happen next. I climbed off him and located my shorts and panties on the floor. I kept my back to him while getting dressed, hoping I was just being paranoid. I was thinking the room was filling with awkward vibes. I could hear and feel Big Baby moving around behind me, so it came as no surprise when my phone started vibrating, signaling that I had a text message. I grabbed the phone, still avoiding eye contact, and read his message. He agreed to give us forty-eight hours to come up with another plan for getting on the ground intel on Royal.

He assured me we could take the next phase of our relationship as slow as I wanted. He loved me and Faith, and we'd always be family. I couldn't deny the warmth he'd just created in me, but I didn't realize how serious it was until I saw a teardrop land on the screen of my phone. For once they weren't tears of sadness. When I finally turned to look at him, he quickly stepped to me and lifted me off my feet, hugging me to his chest tight enough to make me never look for safety anywhere else.

"I love you, too," I whispered, surprised by how much I really meant it more than just friendship.

We continued holding each other for a few minutes, then he set me back on my feet with a look I could easily interpret.

"I'm going to talk to Free, and you can deal with Faith," I said, heading out the door to face the unknown.

It didn't take long to find her sitting on the porch, Face-Timing with somebody.

"Holla at me when you done," I said, preparing to go back inside.

"Oh, nah bitch, bring that ass *here!*"

The demand didn't come out of Free's mouth, but I now knew, who she was Face-Timing with.

"You had to run your mouth, didn't you," I said, smiling regretfully at free.

"You already *know* I did, so get that ass over here like Angel said," Free replied, making room for me to sit on the lounge chair with her.

"It's not a big deal—"

"Don't you lie on my brother's dick like that," Lil' Boy said, from beside Angel on Free's phone.

"Boy bye," I replied, laughing.

Once Angel shooed Lil' Boy out of the room, I braced myself for the interrogation.

"The tea bitch, spill it," Angel demanded.

"I don't even know how it happened, but it happened," I replied, honestly.

"One thing we know for damn sure is that *he* didn't ask for it, so did you just fall on the dick?" Free asked, laughing.

"Fuck you, Freedom, it wasn't like that," I replied, pushing her playfully.

"According to Free it was *exactly* like that because she said she saw that dick *all the way* up in you, and you was on top, too," Angel said.

"Damn bitch, you giving up a play by play? Did you tell her how you almost scared my baby for life because your ass don't know how to knock?" I said, pushing her again.

"Yeah, she told me. All jokes aside, though, you good sis?" Angel asked.

The concern on her face when she asked that question was genuine, and when I looked at Free I saw the same thing.

"Yeah, I'm good. A little sore, but good. It was just so *unexpected,* though."

"So, that was the first time?" Free asked.

"Hell yeah! I ain't never *kissed* that nigga before today, let alone gave up the good-good. It hadn't even crossed my mind some late-night drink and horny type shit," I replied honestly.

"So, what changed?" Angel asked.

It took me a minute to answer that question for myself first, but I had no choice except to acknowledge the truth.

"I realized he's not someone I'm prepared to live my life without, and not just for, Faith either, but for myself. He's my best friend," I confessed, emotionally.

When Free pulled me into her arms I felt those happy tears wanting to overtake me again, but I held them in spite of Angel looking exactly how I was feeling.

"I'm happy for you sis, love is a beautiful thing," Angel said.

"And it's rare too, so hold on to it," Free chimed in.

"You mean that?" I asked, looking up at her.

"Of course, I do, why would you doubt that? You should know by now that I want you to be happy," Free replied, genuinely.

"It's just that I know how you feel about mixing business with pleasure so—"

"And you also know how I feel about being hypocritical. Bitch, I married my best friend. Angel's about to marry hers, so you should know I ain't gonna stop you," Free said.

"Facts," Angel agreed.

"That's why I love you bitches," I replied, smiling.

"Sorry to interrupt," Kamile said, coming out of the house and onto the porch.

"What is it?" Free asked.

"The plan is in play."

Aryanna

Chapter 5
~John Doe~
Guantanamo Bay, Cuba

I was just finishing my second daily regimen of fifteen hundred push-ups when I heard the door open at the end of the hall, and the military police yell attention on deck. This order signaled, that somebody with rank had just stepped into what many people referred to as the devil's playground because if you were locked up here your soul was already lost. I'd sold my soul a long time ago, so I had no worries, only indestructible determination to bring hell to earth, one more time.

"Prisoner eight-four-seven-five-five-nine-eight, Doe, John, step to your pie flap and cuff up," an MP ordered.

I knew the two MPs on duty today were Salazar and Hockley, both were typically laid back so far. One of them told me there was a general outside my door. I knew exactly who it was. I left my shirt off on purpose, as I backed up to the door to be cuffed. Once the handcuffs and leg irons were locked securely, I shuffled forward and took a seat on my bunk. A few seconds later the lock turned, the door was pulled open, and in walked one-star General Madeline Parker. Even in her military dress uniform, with her natural blond hair pulled into a tight ponytail, her five-four, curvy, one-hundred and forty-pound frame still exuded sexiness. Most, if not all of the men she worked with were too intimidated to step to her, but strong women weren't to be feared, they were to be appreciated.

"General Parker, to what do I owe this pleasure?" I asked, sarcastically.

"I'll holler when I'm ready, Salazar," she said, dismissing him and pulling the door shut.

Neither of us said anything until the MPs footsteps had faded away, but our unwavering eye contact said it all.

"Cameras?" I asked.

"Running on a loop, of course, this isn't my first time, John."

"Just making sure. Why are you still way over there?" I asked, standing up.

When she moved away from the door towards me, I turned around, and moments later, I had one hand free from the cold steel of bondage. I turned back to her and took her face in my hands, kissing her softly and passionately, but with enough fire to let her know I'd missed her.

"Well, hello to you, too," she said, breathlessly, once I'd pulled my tongue from her throat.

"It's been a while, I was beginning to wonder if you forgot about me."

"I could never forget about you, you should know that. At the same time, the only way we've been able to keep this thing going for the past two years is by being careful, and not getting greedy," she replied.

I knew she was right, and not just because she was rarely wrong. I knew because where I came from life was built around calculated risks, and survival was afforded to those who didn't try to do too damn much. Me having the balls to step to Madeline wasn't the only thing that had won her over, nor was it my six months of persistent courting her for her attention. It was my ability to be discreet and patient. Both of those things had shown her, that even in this situation. I was about adding to her life, and not risking the career she'd worked so hard for. I couldn't afford to change now, and honestly, she mothered to me too much. For only the third time in my life, I knew love.

"I understand what you're saying sweetheart, and I know you've been missing me, too. Other than that, though, what brought you out from behind your desk?" I asked.

"There's been some developments in the names you've had me keep a lookout for."

Her words had my heart suddenly bumping hard in my chest, but I kept my expression neutral while nodding my head for her to continue.

"The boy doesn't go by Royal Sky anymore, he's now operating under the Walker family name. You would think that would indicate a close family bond, but apparently, nothing could be further from the truth."

"What do you mean?" I asked.

"Well, this is the first time anyone with the name Walker has surfaced since the worldwide manhunt for, Angel Walker, eighteen months ago. About a year ago, Freedom Walker, filed a complaint with the U.S Embassy in Africa because Royal had fled there with her and her other sister's baby."

"Wait, are you saying, Royal, kidnapped two kids?" I asked, in disbelief.

"Not something you'd think an eleven-year-old would be capable of, but apparently his I.Q. is just below genius level, and he inherited the ruthlessness that seems to be a family trait."

"I guess so. What did the U.S embassy do?" I asked, curiously.

"Not a damn thing. He who has the money, the power, and Royal took his sister's money when he took their kids."

"Damn, the boy wasn't playing was he? It sounds like he's trying to provoke his sisters to kill him," I said.

"Given their history, it wouldn't be hard to imagine them killing their own brother. I mean they did kill their own mother, but surprisingly enough they haven't killed him yet. That doesn't mean he's safe, though."

"What do you mean?" I asked.

"Well, I only learned all of this because the Pentagon received credible information linking, Royal, to that huge bombing that leveled the J. Edgar Hoover building awhile back. Isis claimed responsibility, but in the back halls it's been whispered that the timing of it was too coincidental to, Angel Walker's escape."

"So, wait, the United States government actually believes that the Walker sisters engaged in *domestic terrorism* in order to break their sister out?" I asked, skeptically.

"If they've learned anything since their first encounter with anyone named Walker, it's don't underestimate their loyalty. Royal, just seems to be the exception to the rule, and if his sisters really did bomb the F.B.I building they've just painted a target on his back that is not being ignored."

"How solid is the evidence?" I asked, knowing that if the Pentagon was involved shit had to be serious.

"Even with my intelligence clearance, I haven't been able to find that out. I know the U.S. will be looking into this closely, and if Africa's government doesn't cooperate they won't get asked twice."

I didn't have to ask her what that meant because the U.S. government had kept them black OPs boys on the payroll for decades now, and they weren't scared to flash the green light. All this information was interesting if not slightly disturbing, and nothing like I'd anticipated when I told Madeline to be on the lookout.

"What's the time frame before shit gets real?" I asked.

"Yesterday."

"I'm assuming, Royal, bought the government and the Guerrillas, which means he's not easily accessible. What about his sisters, where are they?" I asked.

"No one knows for sure. All anyone knows is that it has to be a country, that won't extradite because anything else would be stupid on their part."

Freedom, Angel, and Destiny could be called a lot of things, but stupid would never be one of them. Even if I didn't know their past, the way they were handling this feud with their brother was a testament to their ability to think outside the box. Hell really had no fury like a woman scorned.

"What do you want me to do?" Madeline asked, looking up at me expectantly.

"Keep your eyes and ears open because a storm is definitely coming."

Aryanna

Chapter 6
~Royal~

"Royal," B.J. said, shaking me awake.

I opened my eyes to find him standing next to my bed, holding Prince's hand. I could tell by the tears on Prince's cheeks that something was going on and that immediately brought me to full alertness.

"What's wrong?" I asked, sitting up and swinging my legs to the floor.

"Prince had an accident," B.J. replied softly, looking at his cousin.

One look at Prince's shorts and the huge wet spot covering them told me everything I needed to know. I hit the call button, by my bed to summon the live-in nanny.

"Did you pee in the bed Prince?" I asked, patiently.

"No, it happened in the bathroom because he couldn't get his shorts down fast enough," B.J. replied.

They may have been cousins, but they were raised as brothers and B.J. was protective of Prince. Even when I understood, I needed to discipline them I couldn't help but love their bond, because I wanted them to depend on each other for life.

"Come here Prince," I said, opening my arms.

He came to me without hesitation, and I picked him up, so I could kiss his little head in understanding before burying his face in my neck and hugging me tightly. It was moments like this when I knew in my heart, that I'd made the right decision taking them with me because my love for them was unconditional. I doubted either of their mothers was capable of that.

"Good morning," Fatima said, from the bedroom doorway.

"Morning, Prince, had a little accident. So, I want you to bathe him, and feed them both, so we can get the day started," I replied, kissing Prince once more before putting him down.

"Not a problem, come on guys," Fatima said, motioning for them to follow her.

Prince took off, but B.J. made sure to get a hug and kiss from me first before running from the room. Once they were gone I nudged the woman sleeping under the covers until she stirred awake.

"Time to get up, I'll call you later," I said, getting up and heading for the shower.

I didn't know her name, but I knew she would be gone by the time I got back, and she'd return when and if I summoned her again. The position I'd carved out for myself since being here allowed me an endless supply of uncomplicated, female companionship whenever I wanted it. I couldn't deny that since entering puberty, I found myself to enjoy using female vocal cords as a catcher's mitt for my semen. I had sex with some of them but raising two kids was enough for me, right now. So, I played it safe. After a refreshing fifteen-minute shower, I returned to my bedroom finding no trace of last night's guest and got ready to attack the days business.

I quickly threw on some blue jeans and a white t-shirt, slid my Timbs on, tucked my pistol into my jeans, and went in search of my own breakfast. One of the most important things I'd learned about having money, was that you didn't necessarily need to always show that you had money. The world was filled with jealous people, and Africa was notorious for its savages. So, most of the time, I moved like a normal person and dressed like it, too. I could've easily afforded to live on one of the more historic palace properties in Nigeria, but instead, I chose a three thousand square foot six-bedroom penthouse condo for us to call home. It definitely wasn't a shack by any means, but it wasn't anything any normal businessman wouldn't have, and I'd established my-self as exactly that in the last year.

"What are you two eating?" I asked, coming into the kitchen.

"Cereal," Prince replied, with his mouth full.

"You want me to get you a bowl?" Fatima offered.

I knew she wasn't trying to treat me like a kid, she was just being polite because that was her nature. Despite her be-ing twenty-four years old, and stunningly beautiful with the softest looking dark skin I'd ever seen. I'd hired her to be the boy's full-time nanny because she was considerate, compas-sionate, and patient. I loved B.J. and Prince to death, but those terrible twos was a bitch some days, and it really did take a village to raise them. I couldn't do it without, Fatima.

"No, I'm good, I'm just gonna make some eggs or some-thing," I replied.

"You not gonna offer to make me none?" She asked, put-ting on her best hurt feelings expression.

I mouthed the words *you're an ass* to her, not wanting to use bad language in front of the kids, and that made her laugh. It was crazy to me how she and I had more of a brother/sister relationship than I ever had with my actual sis-ters, but I enjoyed it.

"You want some eggs for real?" I asked taking every-thing I needed for my three-cheese mushroom omelet out of the refrigerator.

"If you're making omelets then most definitely."

"I got you, but you know you're the only woman I'll cook for," I stated truthfully.

"Don't worry, I made sure to give your overnight guest a blueberry muffin and a bottle of orange juice on her way out the door."

"I always knew you had a heart of gold," I replied, smil-ing.

I could see that she had something smart to say on the tip of her tongue, but the ringing doorbell stopped her. I went to the refrigerator and tapped two buttons to bring up the camera's view from the front door, surprised to see Colonel Fazi here already. It took a numeric code to unlock the front door from the fridges display screen, and once I had it punched in, I used the intercom to let him know I was in the kitchen. I used the few moments it took him to get to the kitchen, to brace myself for whatever bad news he was bringing, because I really didn't anticipate it was good news this early in the morning.

"Good morning, Fazi, you're early," I stated, neutrally.

"I know, but we need to talk."

Fazi wasn't a man to worry over something insignificant, so the look in his eyes right now indicated, that whatever he'd come to discuss with me was beyond serious.

"I'll make the omelet, you take care of business," Fatima insisted, coming around the kitchen counter standing next to me.

"Let's take this to my office," I replied, leading the way down the hall to the room I'd converted.

It was soundproof and impenetrable to even the most advanced listening devices, making it the one and only place, I felt comfortable sharing my innermost secrets and truths. The rooms décor was done in deep rich browns, including the leather swivel chair behind my hand carved, mahogany desk, and the matching leather loveseat that sat against the opposite wall. I had several pieces of art by African painters hanging and two separate sculptures of a mother holding her child. This wasn't just my office, it was my safe place, and I felt stronger here.

"Have a seat," I said, taking my own advice, and preparing myself mentally.

"I received information that some serious questions are being asked about you. The kind of questions that are making the people you pay to look the other way uncomfortable."

I didn't respond immediately, instead, I tried to process what he said and what it meant.

"Before I entertain this conversation, how reliable are your sources that brought this to your attention?" I asked, calmly.

"I wouldn't have come to you without thoroughly vetting both the source and the information, you know that."

"Okay, so what type of questions are being asked, and who's asking them?"

"The questions are about your ties to radical Islamic organizations like Isis, and it's the United States of America doing the asking," he replied, gravely.

"My ties to radical Islamic organizations? I don't *have* ties to terrorists, or anyone perceived to be terrorists because I'm smart enough to know that, that's a bad look. Could they be talking about my diamond mines and the money I provide the Guerrillas to protect my interests?"

"As touchy as Americans are about conflict diamonds, that's not a serious enough issue to get their government involved. I was told this has something to do with the bombing of the F.B.I. building almost two years ago," he replied, looking at me closely.

This piece of information immediately cleared up some of the confusion, but it didn't lessen the sudden apprehension I was feeling.

"I don't know why they're asking about me when it comes to that, that wasn't my handy work," I said, half truthfully.

"Is there any evidence that says differently?" He asked, carefully.

My immediate reaction was to say no, but the truth was I couldn't remember if I'd gotten rid of anything that might've been able to incriminate me. My focus when I left Brazil had been keeping B.J. and Prince safe, but I didn't see how anything I'd done with Black Sam could come to light. Unless…

"Do you know who provided the U.S. authorities with the information that made them start asking questions about me because surely they didn't come to the conclusion that a kid caused that destruction on his own," I said, avoiding his question.

"I do not know where the tip originated from, but they obviously feel like there's some truth to be found or there wouldn't be any questions being asked. For your own protection, I need to know if there is anything to these potential accusations."

"I don't know," I replied, honestly.

Fazi simply stared at me for a moment before rising and going to the small bar I kept in the corner. I didn't drink of course, but I always extended the courtesy to my visitors. Once he had a healthy glass of Bourbon he reclaimed his seat and sipped his drink thoughtfully.

"So, how much money is it gonna take to make the interest in those questions become non-existent for our friends here?" I asked.

"If it were that simple I would have laid that on you from the beginning, but it is going to be more difficult than that I'm afraid."

"What do you mean?" I asked, feeling my apprehension ratchet up another notch.

"The United States of America is a powerful adversary, and the current president is like a child with a toy, only his toy is a nuclear weapon. I'm not saying that a refusal by our government to turn you over to the American authorities would result in all-out war, but I'm not comfortable telling you to test that theory. The American president likes to apply pressure by going after trade and using sanctions that affect countries economically, and our friends would not stand by and allow that to happen."

"Wait, are you implying that the questions being asked, and the pressure being applied is coming from the *president* of the United States?" I asked, skeptically.

"A lot of Federal employees died in that bombing. The F.B.I is considered America's police force, so an attack on them will never be taken lightly."

I knew the truth of what he was saying, and that helped to put my problems into perspective. The only thing I didn't understand was why *I* was having problems.

"Are my sisters under the microscope, too?" I asked.

"Not to my knowledge."

I definitely knew that this wasn't a coincidence, so I turned to my laptop to do some quick digging. I'd learned a lot about hacking from Black Sam before her unfortunate death. I put all my tricks to use in hopes of finding out what was really going on. My search for info started with the F.B.I, but after ten long minutes I came up empty. That meant I had to go deeper. I knew the risks involved with doing that, but it was one risk, I had to take. So, I let my nuts hang and tried to break through the Pentagons firewalls. My adventure lasted all of two minutes before my invasion was detected and my laptop became an expensive paperweight.

"Fuck," I sighed, pushing it off my desk onto the floor.

"My thoughts exactly," Fazi said.

For a moment, I'd forgotten he was still in the room, but I looked up to find him bursting his drink.

"What are my options?" I asked.

"As of now, there has only been questions, not demands, which means you're still safe. When that changes—"

"When that changes, what?" I asked.

"It might be a good idea to think about somewhere else for you and the kids to go."

His statement made a lightbulb go off in my head. This was my sisters play. This was about making it impossible for me to keep B.J. and Prince, because either I would be locked up facing war crimes, or I'd have to run for my life, which was no way for them to live. Kamile had already come running for me, but this plot smelled like Free, and I had to admit the bitch was clever. So, was I though.

"Obviously this could affect my business here, but in the event that I can no longer call Africa home are you willing to protect my interests here?" I asked.

"Of course, I would. When the time comes we can discuss—"

"The time is now. If I wait that would mean playing defense, and that could hurt B.J. and Prince. The smart move is to go on the offensive, which means relocating immediately," I said.

"Where will you go?"

"It's best that you don't know that in case you're asked in a not so nice way. I will keep in touch, though," I promised.

"When do you want to leave?"

"I want to vanish tonight, but we have business to handle before that. I want you to go out to the mines and give everyone a bonus to inspire even more hard work, then I want you to gather one-million in diamonds from our dealer. When you're done with that, I want you to come back here," I ordered.

"I'm on it," he replied, quickly finishing his drink and standing up.

"Send Fatima in on your way out."

He left the room and a few minutes later Fatima came in.

"The boys and I have to leave tonight, and I don't have time to explain all the reasons why. Do you want to come with us?" I asked.

I could tell that my question caught her completely off guard, even though she knew how much I cared about her.

"Will you be coming back?"

"I don't know to be honest. The situation that has me leaving is a serious one, and it might mean that this beautiful place is forever in my rearview. I don't want you to be, though, you're the closest thing to family that I have outside of B.J. and Prince," I confided.

"I know that, and I love you all, but my parents are old—
"

"You don't have to worry about them, I'll make sure they're always taken care of and whenever you want to see them all you have to do is say the word. They can move in here if you want them to," I said, seriously.

"Y—you mean that?"

"Of course, I do. So, will you come with us?" I asked again.

Her eyes were filling with tears, but she was smiling, and I knew that was a good thing.

"Pack light, we've got stops to make."

Aryanna

Chapter 7
~Free~
Four Days Later

"Look, bitch, you're gonna have to stop walking around this damn house with the long face. I know you miss the dick, but Big Baby will be back soon," I said, teasingly.

"Shut up, bitch, it ain't even about the dick! Okay, it's not *all* about the dick," Destiny replied, laughing.

"You know that nigga can take care of himself, and—"

"And Lil' Boy and Bone will always have his back," Angel said, joining us out on the patio.

"I know that, and I appreciate you two letting your dudes go with Big Baby. I know that wasn't easy for you," Destiny replied, genuinely.

She was right, it hadn't been easy, but at the end of the day each one of our men moved like brothers and that meant they went to war together just like we would. Plus, three heads were better than one all day.

"When was the last time you heard from Big Baby?" Angel asked.

"About fifteen minutes ago," Destiny replied.

"She got that nigga on one-hour check-in times," I said, laughing.

"Damn Bitch, you dickmatized already?" Angel asked, laughing right along with me.

"You bitches are soooo funny! It's *not about dick*. I can't stop thinking about the movie *'The Godfather'*," Destiny confessed.

Her admission caused Angel and I to look at each other with the same expression of confusion.

"Okay," I replied, slowly.

"Okay, so, you remember how Brito sent Luca to find out what he could on a rival family after the meeting about getting into the drug business? The next thing you know they get that package with Luca's bulletproof vest with a fish wrapped inside because Luca was sleeping with the fishes. I feel like I just sent Big Baby on that kind of mission," Destiny said.

Again, I looked at Angel, and I could tell she was trying to keep a serious face, but it was only a few seconds later before we were laughing hard enough to bring tears.

"You know what, fuck you, bitches, see if I tell you anything again," Destiny said, fighting a smile.

"I'm-I'm sorry sis, I didn't mean to laugh, but you're overthinking this mission by a lot. First off, Big Baby, didn't go at this alone, and secondly, none of them niggas are going over there trying to infiltrate what, Royal, got going on," I replied, trying to get my laughter under control.

"Plus, if I remember correctly that was right before the war started after Vito got shot. Royal, may have money and power over there, but he damn sure ain't bringing no war our way," Angel chimed in.

"It's my fault for insisting that you watch gangsta movies growing up. I'm sorry," I said, taking Destiny's hand in mine.

"Bitch get off me," Destiny replied, snatching her hand away, laughing.

Despite the serious topic of conversation, it was still good to laugh with my sisters again, because we hadn't been able to do that in recent memory. As badly as my heart ached every day, that my baby boy wasn't with me, for Grace's sake I couldn't wallow in that hurt all the time. That didn't mean I enjoyed life, that simply meant I existed, but having a plan that could actually result in me getting my son back put some warmth into my smile. I knew that the road ahead was long and blanketed in darkness, but I had a reason to hope.

"Can we talk?" Kamile asked, from the open patio doorway.

"Sure," Angel replied, motioning for her to come sit down.

I still hadn't forgiven or forgotten what she'd done, but I understood it, so I pushed it to the back of my mind and focused on the work that needed to be done.

"Okay, so, the hacker I hired was able to manipulate the money trail between the self-driving tractor trailer rental and the ten-million dollars wired to the Middle East, so they showed up on the same Cayman island account. The primary name on the account was Jewel Sky, making Royal the only beneficiary in the event of her death. My people tell me that the Pentagon has already authenticated the account information and strong-armed the Cayman bank, so they were able to follow the money from when Royal drained the account. He's divided it up and hid it well, but he had to keep some close on hand in Africa, which means everything points to him," Kamile reported.

"So, what's next?" I asked.

"The U.S. is probably hours away from demanding that, Royal, be detained and turned over to them immediately, or else. That means the kids will be sent back, too, and Bone and I can go get them," Kamile replied, smiling for the first time in a long time.

I wanted to go get B.J. myself, but being a wanted criminal made that impossible. Thankfully, Bone's name was on our son's birth certificate, and he wasn't wanted for anything.

"What are the odds that Africa refuses to do what the U.S. is asking?" Angel asked.

"With Trump as president, they wouldn't dare," Kamile replied, confidently.

"So, I can tell Big Baby and the fellas to come home," Destiny said, already reaching for her phone.

"Slow down, Destiny, this shit ain't a done deal yet," I said, annoyed because she was clearly only worried about one thing.

Aryanna

The guilty look she gave me told me, she knew she was trippin', which meant I wouldn't have to cuss her ass out.

"So, um, I figured now is probably a good time to tell you that once I have Prince back, I'll be leaving," Kamile said, hesitantly.

"And going where?" Angel asked, quickly.

"I don't really know, yet. I've still got businesses in Russia that'll keep me busy. Or, I was even thinking about going to Japan to see what life is like over there. Maybe we'll just travel the world for a while," Kamile replied, smiling wishfully.

For a second nobody said anything, we all just tried to absorb what was being told to us.

"Why?" I asked, speaking first.

"I just want to spend time with my son and—"

"Don't bullshit us, Kamile, why are you really leaving?" I asked directly.

"If this is about money, I would never take what you've made that's in my accounts," Kamile reassured me.

She knew damn well this wasn't about money, so I didn't even dignify what she'd said with a verbal response. We stared at each other unflinchingly for a long moment until she finally looked away.

"Talk to us Kamile," Angel encouraged.

"It's just that—I-I know you don't want me here," Kamile replied softly.

The Spanish tile covering the patio floor seemed of particular interest to her as she made this statement, but she didn't need to look at me for me to know who she was talking to. It was clear to everyone else, too, because Angel was giving me a look that meant I needed to fix this. Kamile had done some fucked up shit since I'd known her, but one thing she always did was try to make things right. That was admirable because most people fucked up and forgot about it. Reluctantly, I got up from my lounge chair and sat beside her on hers.

"However, brief your relationship was with my dad I've come to believe that your love for him was real and lives on in your love for, Prince. Understanding that slows me to understand why you did what you did, even though, I can't condone it. My love for my father prevents me from killing, Royal, but I will admit it's been a *real* struggle not to. With that being said I want you to know, that I'm working on forgiving you, and I don't want you to take my little brother and leave," I said, genuinely.

"You mean that?" Kamile asked.

"You know damn well, I wouldn't say it if I didn't mean it," I replied.

"Then thank you, Freedom, that means a lot," Kamile said, smiling.

"Yeah, yeah, that don't mean you need to be calling me by my full government name, though," I said, pushing her playfully.

"Yay, you two made up," Angel said, clapping like a really special child.

Her antics made all of us laugh and got rid of any lingering tension.

"Well, now that, that's settled I need to make a store run. Do any of you bitches need anything?" I asked.

"Faith needs apple juice—"

"Oh, get God some too," Angel interjected.

"Anything else?" I asked.

"Can I ride with you?" Kamile asked, warily.

"Yeah, come on," I replied, taking her hand and standing up.

"Pick up something for lunch, too, I'm starving," Destiny said.

I could tell that her demands were about to get out of hand, so I pulled Kamile with me into the house, and out front to my Jeep.

"Do you need to go anywhere besides the grocery store?" I asked once I had us on the move.

"No, I really only came because I wanted a private moment with you. I just wanted to thank you."

"For what?" I asked, looking at her curiously.

"Well, for not killing me even though, I probably deserved it. And for that day on the beach."

That day was something we didn't talk about, it wasn't even something that my sisters knew about as far as I knew. It wasn't my story to tell so I'd always chosen to keep the details to myself. Even without the words, she'd just spoken, I knew she appreciated what I'd done.

"You're welcome," I replied, nonchalantly.

"I've always wondered something, though. Why did you do it?"

Maybe I should've expected this question, but I didn't, and so the only answer that popped into my mind was the truth.

"Because it could've been me on the beach that day," I replied.

"Nah, that *never* would've been you. You're *the* strongest bitch, I know."

"Everybody has their breaking point, Kamile. And while I appreciate that you view me as strong. I know you ain't no weak bitch, yourself. If you can fall into places that dark then anybody can, including me," I stated honestly.

My words left her silent for a while, but I felt like my truth soothed something in her and I was glad for that.

"So, what do you think we should have for lunch today?" I asked, hoping to lighten the mood.

"I don't even know, but—"

Suddenly I felt the steering wheel jump in my hand in response to the truck that had just crashed into the back of me. Luckily, I was able to maintain control of my Jeep, and we were actually on one of the few straight two lane roads leading into town.

"The *last* thing I need is to have to get insurance info from a mufucka that don't speak English!" I said, frustrated and looking for a spot to pull over that wouldn't get me sideswiped.

"You okay?" I asked, glancing over at Kamile.

"I'm fine," she replied, distractedly.

"You sure?"

"Yeah, but don't pull over," she instructed.

"What—why?"

My questions were answered when my rear window shattered, accompanied by the sound of repetitive shots looking for a home. My first thought was crazy because it focused on road rage, but then my survival instincts forced clear analyzation to take over.

"Glove compartment," I yelled, pushing the gas pedal to the floor.

Kamile immediately grabbed the wood handled forty-five, flicked off the safety, turned in her seat, and let loose out the back window. Her shots forced the pick-up truck to fallback quickly because she was aiming straight for the windshield.

"There's an AK-47 in the very back, grab it," I said, after putting some distance between us and the shooter.

Kamile did what I asked without hesitation, climbing back into the passenger seat with the assault rifle and two extra sixty round banana clips.

"Good thing you were prepared," she said, smiling.

"Gotta be, you never know when—"

I was forced to swallow my words as I jumped on the brakes with both feet, sliding the Jeep to a stop not too far from the police roadblock in front of us.

"What the fuck is this," Kamile mumbled.

I was wondering the same thing because four cop cars making the road impassable, along with eight cops standing out in the open with their guns drawn, wasn't a sight seen regularly. Something was up, and it smelled foul.

"No sudden movements. Pass me the gun real slow, get your phone out, and text Destiny," I said, slowly, trying not to move my lips.

"Evacuation plan A?"

"Yep," I replied, accepting the gun and carefully pulling the slide back to engage the first bullet.

Suddenly, one of the cops yelled something in Spanish that I didn't understand.

"Did you get that?" I asked, making sure to keep my eyes locked on the action in front of us.

"Yeah, they want us to get out of the car. Now."

"Somehow that seems like a bad idea from where I'm sitting," I said.

"On that, we agree. I just sent the text to Destiny, so we really need to stall for a couple minutes so she can get the kids down to the boat."

Having to run at a moment's notice was a reality we'd accepted long ago, even though, Brazil had no laws of extradition with the United States. Foreign governments could be bought or bullied, and us being at the mercy of that wasn't an option. We kept a speedboat docked not far from the house, and a small yacht anchored about forty-five minutes out at sea, but traveling with kids meant it wasn't a hop, skip, jump situation. The fact that the cop was yelling at us again spoke to their impatience.

"He's saying get out or they'll shoot," Kamile translated.

"I get the feeling that's what they wanna do anyway," I said, slowly putting the Jeep into reverse.

When I glanced briefly in the rearview mirror, I saw that the truck that had been shooting at us had just crept around the bend, and it was now blocking the road behind us.

"How many bullets you got left in the pistol?" I asked.

"Four I think."

"Use them," I said, mashing my foot down on the gas while bringing the AK up and letting that bitch breathe through the windshield.

Chaos erupted instantly as they fired back, but I didn't take my foot off the gas or my finger off the trigger. Luckily, I'd built up enough momentum that when I rammed the truck trying to box us in it was tossed to the side like old fruit.

"Hope they had their seatbelts on," I said sarcastically, spinning the steering wheel and quickly throwing the truck in drive.

It wasn't until I went to pass the gun to Kamile that I saw the look on her face and the blood on her shirt. I could tell she was in shock, but that was better than being dead.

Aryanna

Chapter 8
~Angel~

"I'm telling you now, bitch, you're *so* lucky I love you because your daughter's pull-up smelled like something crawled up in there and *died*," I said, trying to inhale as much fresh air as I could.

"Stop acting like I ain't changed some of the bombs God's little nasty behind drops, and you *know* that boy be rotten."

I couldn't deny that. All I could do was laugh at the face Destiny was making because it looked like she has smell recall.

"Whatever, bitch, I thought Faith was potty trained," I said, sitting back down on the lounge chair next to her.

"She is, but sometimes she has accidents in her sleep, which is why she still wears pull-ups."

"I've tried potty training, God, but that little boy is so damn stubborn! I told Lil' Boy that he must get that shit from him because that ain't me."

"Sure, you're not stubborn at all," Destiny replied, with heavy sarcasm.

"Fuck you!" I said, laughing and pushing her playfully.

When her phone started chirping it immediately snatched her undivided attention as she began frantically searching for it.

"Look at you, your ass is *sprung*!" I teased, laughing at her hurried movements.

The smile on her face when she finally found her phone told me, I was right about her yearnings for Big Baby's loving, but whatever she read erased that smile in seconds.

"Evacuate," she said, looking at me.

"Evacuate? You're sure?"

Aryanna

"Positive, I'll get the kids and you grab what we need," she said, already moving.

I had no idea what the fuck had happened in the few minutes that Kamile and Free had been gone, but for us to be leaving meant it was *all* bad. I immediately ran from room to room collecting all the laptops and stored them in a fireproof travel case that required either mine or one of my sister's fingerprints to open. Once that was done, I went to the safe Free kept in her closet and emptied its contents into a duffle bag, then I did the same for the one in Destiny's room. I quickly put the bags and carrying case outside on the patio and ran to the front door. After setting the alarm I grabbed the bag with the two Mossberg pumps, the UZI, and extra ammo out of the hall closet, and met Destiny back on the patio.

"I'll stay with them, go grab the Range Rover," I said, tossing her the keys.

Just as she disappeared from sight, my phone started going off, forcing me to put the bag of guns down and dig it out of my pocket. I was expecting it to be Free or Lil' Boy, but instead it was an alert that the motion detectors positioned a half a mile away were going off. I quickly pulled up the video footage and caught sight of a line of Brazilian police cars headed in our direction. Since the security system was linked to all our phones, I knew everyone was seeing the same images I was at this moment. No doubt they were sick to their stomachs too.

"God, I want you to take your cousin's hand and walk down the stairs over there," I said, pointing to the spot where Destiny had just slid my truck to a stop.

Thankfully, both children did exactly as they were told, which allowed me to carry a sleeping Grace in her car seat, and one of the duffle bags. We quickly got the kids buckled in, got everything thrown in the truck, and fled down the beach. We'd only made it about two hundred feet away when the house we'd considered a safe-haven exploded in action movie fashion, rocking the Range Rover from side to side. The house had been rigged to blow fifteen seconds after the front door was opened, which meant some people had definitely lost their lives in the giant fireball I could see in my rearview mirror.

"Well, one thing we know for damn sure is that Free wasn't just being paranoid," I said, driving faster.

"Neither was I. This is obviously an act of war."

"Yeah, but how the fuck would, Royal, get the police in Brazil to come after us?" I asked.

"I don't know, but we managed to make the U.S. government go after him."

"Touché," I replied, checking my rearview to see if there was any pursuit on the sand behind us. Even though, I didn't see anyone I still pushed the gas down harder because I could see the boat dock ahead in the distance.

"Brother or no brother, I'm starting to feel like this little nigga needs killing," Destiny said seriously.

Looking at all our kids in the backseat made me feel exactly as she did because this stunt Royal pulled had put all of them in danger. There was no way we could give him the opportunity to do that again.

"As soon as we get to safety we're gonna put that shit to a vote, but I'm telling you now, I'm leaning towards your way of thinking."

"After this shit, it shouldn't be hard to convince, Free either," she replied.

When I brought us to a stop at the docks we both hopped out, moving with purpose because we didn't know if the police knew that the sleek black speedboat belonged to us.

"Kids first," I said, grabbing Grace's car seat and taking God by the hand.

Somehow Grace had slept through the massive explosion, but the rear of the boat's engine was sure to disrupt her peaceful slumber.

"You stay with them and get the boat started, but don't untie it," I said, before taking off back down the dock towards my truck at a dead run.

After pulling the Uzi and an extra clip out of one bag, I loaded myself down with as much as I could carry and made my way back to the boat.

"There's Free and Kamile," Destiny said, pointing behind me.

I quickly dropped everything except the gun and headed back in the direction of the Jeep that had just slid to a stop behind my Range Rover. As I ran, I made sure to keep my eyes open for anyone coming from any direction because now that Free and Kamile had arrived anyone else could only be an enemy.

"The kids and everything are already on the boat," I yelled, grabbing the last duffle bag from the truck, and throwing it around my shoulder so I could still have my hands full of firepower.

When I saw Free step out of her Jeep with blood all over her I froze, gripped by a fear I couldn't put into words.

"Help me," she demanded, scrambling around to the passenger side of the Jeep. Seeing her move allowed me to move because it was obvious the blood wasn't hers.

"How bad is it?" I asked, as soon as I got to her side.

"She's been hit twice in the chest, just above her heart. She lost consciousness a few minutes ago," Free replied, easing Kamile out of the passenger seat.

I quickly slung the uzi around my shoulder and grabbed Kamile's feet to balance out Free grabbing her upper body.

"Fuck!" Kamile screamed, in pain as we began moving with her down the dock.

Having been shot myself, I knew how much she was hurting, right now, but the good news was she was still alive. Thankfully, by the time we'd made it to the boat Destiny had already hidden the children in the bedroom, so they didn't have to see this shit.

"Destiny, untie us so we can get the fuck out of here," I demanded.

"Wait!" Free exclaimed.

"What, what is it?" I asked once we had Kamile laid across the seat in the back of the boat.

"I gotta get the guns out of my Jeep, I know we hit some cops in that shootout," Free replied, hopping back onto the dock and sprinting towards her Jeep.

It wasn't until she was halfway there that I saw the first cop car crest the top of the hill, heading straight towards her.

"Free!" I screamed, running after her.

She didn't stop or turn around, but I could tell by her increase in pace that she'd seen the same thing I did. Leave it to her crazy ass to think she could outrun a car, and to her credit she almost did. *Almost.* I could tell, she would get to her Jeep at the same time the cops would reach the bottom of the short hill, leaving them no more than ten feet apart. I couldn't take the chance that they'd get a clean shot at her, so I raised the uzi and fired on the run. My shots had the desired effect of halting their forward progress, but I didn't take my finger off the trigger until they were reversing as quick as they'd come.

"Come on!" I screamed at Free, changing clips and keeping watch like a sentinel from the end of the dock.

Within seconds she had what she'd come for and was back on the run towards me. I backpedal halfway down the dock before turning and running full speed after her. By the time, I'd untied us from the dock and hopped back in the boat the beach behind us was crawling with cops. Destiny immediately went below to keep the children calm while I took the wheel, and Free kept pressure on Kamile's wounds. Moments later, I had us moving at a high rate of speed far beyond the laws reach, making it to the forty-five-minute rendezvous point in under thirty minutes.

Once we made it to the yacht Kamile had bought a year ago we carried her aboard and hid her away in the main suite where we could look after her without the kids seeing. We got everything loaded up, including the kids, then filled the speedboat with enough bullet holes to have it halfway under water before the yacht started moving. I left Destiny with the task of getting the kids settled and I joined Free with Kamile.

"How is she?" I asked, entering the room quietly.

"She's lost a lot of blood, but it looks like the bullets tore straight through."

"Destiny somehow got a doctor to agree to meet us in intercontinental waters. We've just gotta keep her alive until then," I said, looking down at a pale Kamile.

She'd spent so many moments by my side when I was laid up unconscious, I owed her the same in return. I just wished the situation had never occurred for me to be able to pay her back.

"What the fuck happened, Free?" I asked, sitting on the bed on the other side of Kamile.

"I was driving, and a truck tapped my bumper. Next thing I know we're getting shot at and running right into a police barricade, but luckily I keep tools on deck."

"Did the cops say anything, I mean the U.S. has no jurisdiction to send them at us, but obviously that's what happened," I said.

"The only thing they told us was to get out or get shot, and you can see what we chose. We don't know for sure that it was the U.S. government that sent the cops at us though, and honestly, I don't think it was."

"What makes you so sure?" I asked, curiously.

"Because we're fugitives and the U.S. have fugitive apprehension teams or U.S. Marshalls at the very least. If they knew our exact location, they wouldn't send the locals because they'd already view them as incompetent for not discovering us first. The U.S. government would've come at us with precision, not the rush job that was more like a botched hit instead of an arrest attempt."

"So, you think it's, Royal?" I asked.

"That's the safe bet, I mean we've benefited from Brazil's corruption for a while now, so we know it exists. It makes sense that he'd come at us, which means he knows about what we've done. The only question is whether or not he's in custody."

Her statement made me reach for the phone in my pocket, so I could call Lil' Boy, and based on the fifty missed calls I had, accompanied by the same amount of text messages, I was long overdue.

"Babe, it's me," I said, once he answered.

I immediately had to snatch the phone away from my ear because he started yelling. It took a good thirty seconds before I could get a word in. Once I did I patiently explained to him that he needed to listen to me without interruption. I then proceeded to tell him everything that had happened since all hell broke loose, including Free's theory about Royal being behind everything. Surprisingly, Lil' Boy took the bad news better than I'd thought he would, then he delivered some bad news of his own. We agreed on a meeting spot that we were both familiar with, said our '*I love yous*', and disconnected.

"Did you just tell your man that we'd meet him in Russia?" Free asked, looking at me like I'd finally lost it.

"Yeah, well be safe there."

"Have you forgotten that President Trump is best friends with Puttin?" she asked.

"They're not best friends, Trump's his bitch, and it'll stay that way because Puttin knows where all the dirty little secrets are. He doesn't owe Trump any favors, and he damn sure won't be giving him any as long as he's still collecting tribute from Kamile's businesses. Trust me, we'll be safe," I insisted.

"I hope you're right because you really can't afford to be wrong. What else did Lil' Boy say?"

I knew there was no easy way to give Free bad news except to give it to her, but I still hesitated for a moment.

Aryanna

"By the time, the Nigerian authorities agreed to cooper-ate with the United States request to hand, Royal over, he and the kids were long gone. No one knows where yet," I replied, softly.

We sat in silence for a moment, listening to the shallow breathing of Kamile, hoping she'd continue to hold on for as long as it took to get her to a doctor. I could feel the heavi-ness of Free's thoughts and I knew the decision she was weighing in her mind. The promise she'd made to our father was one she probably never thought she'd have to break, but Royal might've pushed her too far.

"Lil' Boy told me one more thing. He thinks they found something that might draw Royal out, but it could mean get-ting more blood on our hands," I said.

Free looked at me, then looked back down at Kamile be-fore she spoke.

"More blood on my hands ain't a problem as long as it doesn't belong to anyone I love. They've bled enough."

Chapter 9
~Destiny~
Two days later

"Finally," I sighed in relief, leaping into Big Baby's arms as soon as he came through the cabin door.

"Daddy!" Faith yelled, attacking his legs with her little arms and legs, wrapping herself around his lower body.

This was one of the times I was glad he couldn't talk because my only interest in communication involved me sticking my tongue down his throat. I kissed him with a fierce passion and possession, desperate to convey how much I missed him even though, it had only been a few days. I'd almost lost my life in those days, and we'd almost lost our chance at what our love could blossom into. His enthusiasm with regards to how tightly he held me, and how deeply he fell into my kiss, told me he was feeling everything I was.

"Up daddy, up," Faith cried, trying to pull us apart, so she could get to him.

Ordinarily, I would've moved out of her way, but I needed the life he was breathing into me, right now.

"Da-ddy!" Faith whined, indicating she was moments away from a full-blown tantrum.

We shared a few more sweet kisses before he put me back on my feet and picked up his little girl, much to her delight and my annoyance. After several moments of kisses and tickling he was allowed to put her down, so she could return to her coloring book on the floor, and we took a seat on the queen-sized bed.

"Are you okay?" I asked, looking him over as closely as he was me.

He nodded his head that he was fine, taking my hand in his and kissing it softly. There was so much I wanted and needed to say, but instead, I folded myself into his welcoming embrace and we watched our daughter color. The uninterrupted hour we spent listening to Faith babble as the boat rocked us soothingly was better than any vacation I'd ever been on in my life. I hadn't known peace like this since I'd been with Black Sam, and I was surprised it came without the guilt, I thought would accompany any attempt I made to move past my grief.

Maybe it was because even though this thing between Big Baby and me was new, the love and comfort we shared was battle tested. A love between best friends was the definition of epic. A knock on the door finally interrupted on our family time, but we both understood there was plenty of work to do.

"Yeah?" I called out.

"Meet us in the dining room after you take, Faith, to my room," Free said, from outside the door.

As badly as I wanted to stay exactly where I was, I reluctantly got up.

"Come on, Faith, let's go find your cousins," I said.

"Is daddy going?"

I looked at Big Baby in response to her question, knowing that our daughter didn't want him out of her sight anymore than I did. He gave me a knowing smile before moving to pick her up.

"Free's room is at the end of the hall, and you can meet us upstairs once you have her distracted," I said, opening the door for them to leave.

I moved down the hall in the opposite direction, taking the stairs up to the yachts main level where I found everyone except Kamile sitting around the massive glass table. Thankfully, the doctor we'd paid one-hundred thousand dollars managed to save Kamile's life and sew her up, but she was still heavily sedated because the pain was no joke. Despite her good standing as a businesswoman in Russia, her being shot was why we'd all agreed to stay on the yacht in Port instead of venturing into Moscow. No one wanted the questions that came with gunshot victims. Life on a five-stateroom, the one-hundred-foot yacht wasn't hard living by any means, especially since it stayed fully stocked and operated on a two-person six-month skeleton crew. For us, it was the perfect place to hide and plan our next move.

"I'm almost as happy to see you two as I was Big Baby," I said addressing Lil' Boy and Bone, sitting down across from them.

"You saying almost doesn't hurt my feelings at all," Lil' Boy replied, sarcastically.

"Aww, you know I still love you, bruh, probably more now because you brought your brothers back in one piece," I said.

"He knew not to let nothing happen to Bone or he would've had to deal with Free," Angel said, seriously.

"Ain't nothing gonna happen to me, and besides we were safer in Africa than if we'd have stayed at home with you all," Bone replied, looking across the table directly at his wife.

"How's Kamile?" I asked.

"She'll live, but she can't be involved in whatever comes next," Free replied.

"And what's next?" Angel asked.

At that moment, all eyes turned on Free because we knew this had to be her call, her decision to live with the consequences once she rung that bell. When I looked at her, I expected to find some hint of the internal struggle she had to be dealing with, but I didn't see any of that. All I saw was determination, and I knew what her decision was.

"Our next move is to go after, Royal. The fact that the U.S. government is looking for him makes him a wounded animal and there's really nowhere he can hide for long. We just need to find him first," Free stated, calmly.

"A wounded animal is the most dangerous kind," Bone commented.

"No more dangerous than a mother protecting her young," Free replied.

"Are you sure about this?" Angel asked, carefully.

I knew Angel could see the same resolve in our sister that everyone else at the table could, but still, she had to ask because we all knew going down this path ensured only one end.

"Yeah, I'm sure," Free replied, without hesitation.

After those words we all nodded our heads, knowing that Royal had just made the transition from Father-God's son to just another nigga who'd get a closed casket courtesy of us.

"We've got his nanny's parents bound and gagged in one of the rooms downstairs, and they're still insisting they don't know where Fatima took off to," Lil' Boy said.

"Is there any doubt that she's with, Royal?" I asked.

"No, Royal, may not be the average teenager, but he's not capable of running and caring for two toddlers on his own," Bone said.

"Is there no theory on where he might be headed?" Free asked.

"No, we questioned his right-hand man, Colonel Fazi, till death was the only option, and all we learned is that Royal, is traveling with a million dollars, worth of diamonds. Fazi, also confirmed that it was his associates in Brazil that came after you all," Lil' Boy replied.

"I'm sure you made him regret that decision," I commented.

"Many times over," Bone assured.

"How is he traveling?" Free asked.

"The last Fazi saw was by freighter, but Royal, wouldn't tell him any destination in case he was questioned. We do know he has fake papers," Lil' Boy replied.

"Smart fucker," Angel said, shaking her head.

"How do Fatima's parents communicate with her?" Free asked.

"She left them three different numbers for different burn phones, informing them that each would only be good for one call, but she'd provide them with a new number during each call," Bone stated.

"Smart fuckers," I mumbled.

"Okay, so it's obvious that Fatima is someone, Royal, trusts or he wouldn't have kept her around, let alone taken her with him. She's the weak link, and we need to draw her out to get to him," Free said.

"How do you want to do that?" Bone asked.

The sound of the slide being pulled back on a pistol and a round being chambered pulled all our attention to the doorway leading to this dining room. There stood Big Baby with an all-black .50 caliber Desert Eagle gripped firmly in his hand, looking directly at Free with the answer to Bone's question clear in his eyes.

"We're on the same page Big Baby, but it needs to be done quieter because there are other boats around. And the kids are on board," Free said.

"Maybe we should push out to sea if you're planning to kill them because we've gotta get rid of the bodies afterward," Angel suggested.

"You're right, but we're not killing both of them because we gotta keep one for leverage," Free replied.

"Which one?" I asked.

"Let's go find out," Free said, standing up.

"I'll go tell the captain to get us moving," Lil' Boy offered.

The rest of us filed downstairs and into the stateroom at the opposite end of the hall from the children. There was an older black couple laying forehead to forehead on the bed, seemingly asleep, but our presence immediately made them open their eyes.

"Remove their gags," Free instructed Big Baby.

Once that was done she stood at the foot of the bed and addressed them.

"Your daughter is employed by the person who kidnapped my son and my brother, and I need to find them before something bad happens," Free said.

"That is a lie, Royal, would never harm the children. He loves them," the man stated, confidently.

"I'm not here to debate with you, I'm here so you can help me find your daughter, and just to prove that I'm *not* a liar, I'll tell you some more truth. You're both gonna die," Free confessed, emotionlessly.

There was no quick response from the man this time, only the soft cries from the woman lying next to him.

"Please y-you don't have to—"

"But I do, I do have to because getting those innocent kids back safely means more to me than your life ever could," Free said.

"We don't-don't know where they are," the woman sobbed.

"That's not the information I came to get. I need to know which one of you is Fatima's favorite parent?" Free asked, seriously.

I had no idea if the couple knew where this line of questioning would lead, but I damn sure did, and it was bad for both of them. I was sure that in their heart of hearts they were at this very moment convincing themselves that this polite, soft-spoken woman wouldn't kill them as she'd threatened to do. They just didn't realize that the soft-spoken, polite side of Free was as an indicator that beast mode was right around the next corner.

"Fatima loves us both and would be heartbroken to lose either of us. Please don't do this," the woman begged.

"It's not me who's doing this, it's the person your husband tried defending and insulted me for," Free replied.

"I did not mean to insult you, *please* let my wife and I go."

"Can't do it, so I'm gonna ask you one last time, which one of you is Fatima's favorite?" Free asked, calmly.

This time neither of them replied, but I knew that wouldn't save them anymore than begging for their lives had. Suddenly, I felt the yacht moving, which meant Fatima's parents were running out of time.

"If one of you doesn't tell me the truth in the next thirty seconds, you'll be watching the person you love die by my hand," Free promised.

Still, neither of them uttered a word or moved, they simply continued to look deeply into each other's eyes like all the answers to life's abnormalities were hidden within each other. It was sweet, but still not a deterrent for Free.

"The man first," Free said,

Big Baby lifted the slim built man like he was made of feathers and tossed him at Free's feet.

"Bone make sure she watches, and Big Baby get me a sharp knife," Free demanded, pulling the man upright by his throat.

His wife was on the verge of hysteria, speaking rapidly in her native tongue while Bone held her head in a vise grip facing Free. When Big Baby returned with the butcher knife and passed it to Free I expected the woman to close her eyes, but instead, she looked on and her ramblings took on a chanting cadence.

"Destiny, get your phone out, stand next to Bone and videotape what I do to him. When I'm done I want you to turn the phone towards Fatima's mother," Free instructed.

I did as she asked, signaling to her when I started recording.

"Fatima, I'm sure you don't know me, or the whole story about how the thirteen-year-old boy you're traveling with came to be the guardian of two small boys. He kidnapped them. B.J. is my son and Prince is my brother. I want them both returned to me safely. I don't care what lies, Royal, told you, or that you've believed them up until this point. What I care about is those children, and that you understand every word I speak to you will be the truth. If you do not help me get those children back, I'm going to kill both of your parents. To prove that I mean what I say, I'm going to slit your father's throat now," Free stated, coldly.

Within seconds she delivered on her promise, filling the room with the sounds of the woman screaming next to me and her husband gargling his life's essence. Free's expression never changed while the man in front of her bled out, and when it was clear he was gone she let his body drop in front of her.

"I promise you that your mother will die slower. The choice is yours," Free said, nodding towards me.

I quickly turned my phone on the completely devastated woman for a full ten seconds before shutting the recording off. I played it back to make sure I had captured everything and watching it all unfold the second time made me shudder. Free had never looked so detached and menacing before, and it was clear that taking B.J. had pushed her to another level of malicious intent.

"What do you want me to do with the video?" I asked.

"Get with Lil' Boy and send it to all of Fatima's burner phones. Make sure you tell her that she has twenty-four hours."

Chapter 10
~John Doe~

"Two visits in a week means I'm special or you have news that couldn't wait," I said, once Madeline closed my cell door behind her.

"Actually, it's both, but since I had to leave sooner than I wanted to last time we're gonna start with pleasure, before business," she replied, quickly crossing the cell to me, and snatching my shorts down.

I could tell by the smile on her face she was glad I wasn't wearing any underwear. Her hands immediately went to my dick, gripping it firmly enough to wake it from its slumber.

"Cuffs," I said, desperately wanting my hands loose, so I could use them to navigate the beautiful landscape of her body.

"There's no time," she replied, pushing me down on my bunk before quickly unbuttoning her pants, and pushing them to the floor so she could step out of them.

I didn't have time to admire her black lace bikini panties, but once she straddled me, I definitely appreciated that they were crotchless. When she took me inside of her, the sight of pleasure that tumbled from her mouth only added to my arousal, making my dick throb harder within her tight fortress.

"God, I n-needed this," she confessed, moving her hips rapidly and making it clear she was on a mission. I loved the dominating side of her, but at this pace, I knew I wouldn't last long.

"Baby, slow-slow down," I panted.

Her response was to silence me in kisses as she rode me faster and harder, squeezing her pussy tighter around my dick with every motion. The fight to keep my eyes focused on the woman over top of me and off the back of my eyelids was real because she was coaxing my climax with a swiftness only reserved for virgins. Somehow, I managed to hold on until I felt her body buck against mine with the force of a wild horse, and then her pussy gripped me in a way that made my resistance run for cover. Like the beauty of a tropical storm, we came together as quietly as we could, and she laid on my chest long after I'd stopped pulsating inside her.

"Did I-Did I hurt you?" She asked, fighting for air.

"Only my pride, but I'll get over it."

She kissed me quickly, climbed off me, and put her pants back on. By the time I struggled into a sitting position she was back in front of me to help pull my shorts back up, but first, she licked and slurped all the flavors of us off my dick.

"You're gonna make me hard again," I warned, wishing I could wrap my fingers in her hair and make love to her face.

"I owe you some more of that the next time I see you, which I'm anticipating will be sooner than later after we talk."

I wasn't exactly sure how to take her comment, but she had my attention.

"What's going on?" I asked, sliding my hands behind my back in hopes of decreasing the numbness and restoring blood flow.

"A lot's going on, and it's not good. Royal, has officially been named a fugitive by the U.S. government, and I found out that the evidence they have against him is a money trail. It's solid too."

"The African government won't hand him over, though, right?" I asked.

"Wrong. They fully intended to give him up to avoid the trade war and tariff tax that the President threatened to hit their country with, but he found out the law was looking for him, and when he fled, he must've figured out it was his sisters that set him up. The working theory is that he made a move against them."

"Working theory based on what? I thought nobody knew where the Walker sisters were hiding?" I replied, not liking the feeling of where this was going.

"You're right nobody knew, but Royal obviously had to if he kidnapped their kids. A couple days ago in Brazil, all hell broke loose when the police tried to apprehend some international fugitives they'd been tipped off about. That's the official story that was given to explain a shootout with the police and a house exploding."

"Wait, what?" I asked, trying to wrap my mind around what she was saying.

"You heard me correctly, and fifteen Brazilian cops lost their lives. A closer inspection revealed that these cops were suspected of being dirty, and we know who had the most recent motive to send dirty cops at the Walker sisters."

"But how do you even know it was them? Did-did one of them die or get caught?" I asked, hesitantly.

"No, no one died that we know of, but one of their associates was wounded. When Angel Walker was captured almost two years ago after being in that car bomb she only had one visitor while she was in the hospital, and the woman was listed on all of Angel's paperwork as her sister. It wasn't Freedom or Destiny, and it's now known that it wasn't her sister at all, but a woman named Kamile Armstrong."

I made sure to keep my face completely neutral after hearing this revelation, but my heart was hammering in my chest harder than it had been when Madeline was on top of me.

"So, this Kamile Armstrong, who is she and where is she?" I asked.

"She's actually a legitimate cushiness woman who started out as a stripper. No criminal record, but she obviously has criminal ties. She's been wanted for questioning since Angel's disappearance, but no one knew where she was until her blood was found in a Jeep with hers and Freedom's prints all over it."

"Her blood," I replied, fighting to keep my tone and voice infliction normal.

"Yeah, her blood, and it was a lot of it. We wouldn't have known that it was her if her DNA hadn't been on file from her baby's birth."

"B-baby, she has a baby—how old?" I asked, rapidly.

"Yeah, she has a baby boy that's almost two years old. He's the one Royal took, along with Freedom's son," she replied, slowly, looking at me differently.

My recovery to this piece of information was as swift as my calculations, and my math was only adding up to one solution.

"So, basically Royal is out to kill his sisters and vice versa," I concluded.

"Right, which means we need to implement the plan we talked about."

"Madeline are you sure? Because once this thing goes hypothetical there's no turning back. Life as you know it will change forever," I warned.

"My life was forever changed the first time we ever had a conversation, and I've never regretted a single moment we've spent together since. In my heart, this feels like my happily ever after, despite the circumstances. The only way that dream can be fully realized is if we continue on the path we're on," she replied, sealing her commitment with a soft kiss. Her words were music to my ears and they allowed hope to swell within me for the first time in a long time. I felt reborn.

"I'm with you sweetheart, all you have to do is what we discussed before."

Chapter 11
~Royal~
One Week Later
Jamaica

"Royal, we're hungry."

I looked up from the laptop screen I'd been trapped inside for at least the last hour to find B.J. and Prince standing next to me, holding hands.

"Why didn't you tell, Fatima?" I asked.

"I did, but she won't get up," B.J. replied, sullenly.

His response frustrated me because I knew, I'd have to stop what I was doing and tend to them, which was what I'd brought Fatima along for.

"Okay, I'll order you some food, just go watch T.V. until it gets here," I instructed, rising from my seat at the desk, going to the phone by the bed.

After ordering three hamburgers and french fries from room service, I went to the second bedroom in our suite in search of Fatima. As usual, I found her face down in bed.

"Why didn't you feed B.J. and Prince?" I asked, impatiently.

"I told them to give me a minute and I would."

"They're hungry *now,* though. Since when is that not a priority to you?" I asked.

"Since we've had to hop from continent to continent in the last week, and I've barely slept. Madrid, Italy, London, Paris, and now, Jamaica. Non-stop movement is *exhausting,* Royal."

"I understand that, but I can't apologize for it. We had to stay on the move until I was sure that we weren't being followed."

"And you're sure of that now?" She asked, sitting up slowly, turning to face me.

Aryanna

I could see the fatigue in the red lines clouding her eyes, and it inspired guilt where frustration had just existed within me. I knew Fatima had no idea what she'd signed up for when she'd agreed to come with us, but neither had I for real. Running from someone you perceived as your enemy on a street level was one thing but running from the most powerful government in the known world was another. My dear sisters had done a wonderful job trying to box me in. The only problem was they'd somehow forgotten that when you put a cat in a corner he came out scratching. They'd just barely gotten away in Brazil, but they wouldn't be so lucky next time. *If* I could concentrate on putting a plan together.

"I don't think we've been followed, but we still have to be extremely cautious. We won't be moving in the next few days, though, so you should be able to get some rest, okay?" I replied.

"Whatever you say. Where are the boys? I'll get them something to eat," she said, standing up.

"I already ordered their food one benefit of hotel living."

"That's true. Well since you've got that handled, I'm going to take a shower," she said, walking past me and into her bathroom.

I returned to my laptop and the search I'd been doing for my sister's whereabouts, but Fatima stayed on my mind. Past tired and fatigue, I'd seen sadness in her eyes as well. I knew that was due to her being homesick and missing her parents. I knew that pain intimately because not a day passed that I didn't miss my mother. In my heart, I knew that life on the run was no way for B.J. and Prince to live, but the thought of what my sisters had done to the woman who'd given them life continued to strengthen my resolve.

They were bad people, incapable of the nurturing love, every little boy needed from his mom, the love I'd been given every day of my life. Until they'd taken it away from me. No matter how tough the situation was for me and the little guys right now, I still knew it was better than the life they would've had if I would've left them. A knock at the door signaled the arrival of lunch, and once I had them settled in front of the T.V. watching cartoons with their food I took my food back to my bedroom where I could work and eat. An hour later, my frustration had returned because my search was coming completely empty.

The Brazilian authorities had no idea where they'd disappeared to, hell, for all they know my sisters could've simply moved to another hideout somewhere further off the grid in Brazil. They were obviously too smart to leave a footprint or trail of any kind to be followed, but that didn't surprise me as much as it angered me. Knowing their location had given me an advantage, but now the playing field was leveled because I couldn't fight what I couldn't see. It was still another thirty minutes before my growing frustration forced me to concede victory. I did receive some good news in the form of an email from the private security firm I hired alerting me of their arrival in Jamaica.

Even in Kingston being as nice as it was one could never be too careful while traveling with the number of diamonds I had in my possession. The truth was that the diamonds, and the story I'd told about being African royalty, were simply excuses to have hired guns at my disposal. I'd paid handsomely for those guns to ask no questions, and to shoot in any direction I pointed. I replied to their email with the name of the hotel we were staying at and told them to set up a perimeter and wait for further instructions. After that was taken care of, I decided that some fresh air might do me some good, and the beach was close enough to make that destination appealing.

"I'll be back," I said, walking past Fatima and the boys sitting together on the couch.

"Wait, where are you going?" She asked, hopping up and blocking my access to the front door.

"Just out for a walk."

"Well, I need to talk to you, and I've been waiting because I didn't want to interrupt you," she said.

"I won't be gone long."

When I went to move past her she blocked my way again and stood there with her arms crossed over her chest with a look on her face that I knew well.

"Are you really saying that whatever you wanna talk to me about can't wait?" I asked, seriously.

Her response was to grab me by the hand and pull me back towards my bedroom. I resigned myself to hearing her out and took a seat on my bed.

"What's wrong?" I asked.

"Royal this is hard for me. I mean you know I love B.J., Prince, and you, but this situation is still hard for me to be in. I don't even know why we're *running*."

It had been my plan to tell her what was going on, but I had yet to find the right words to explain my legal entanglements or the situation with my sisters. Part of me feared that Fatima would see my actions as kidnapping, and therefore unjustifiable, which could make her question my judgment. That wasn't something I wanted or needed, right now.

"It's complicated," I replied, vaguely.

"No shit it's complicated, but I need to know how much more complicated it can get. What I'm asking is, am I in danger?"

"No, you're not in danger. I'll always keep you safe," I promised.

"Keeping me safe isn't the same as not being in danger, Royal, you know that."

"Have I ever lied to you?" I asked, sincerely."

"No, not that I know of."

"Okay, then, I'm not about to start lying to you now. You're not in any danger," I said convincingly, standing up to show that I was done with this conversation.

"I trust you, it's just that I'm homesick and I don't know what to do. I feel so lonely," she confessed.

"I understand that you miss your parents, but you shouldn't feel lonely because you have me and the boys."

"Do you mean that, do I really have you?" She asked, looking at me as if she intended to look through me.

"Of course, you do, why would you even question that?"

For a moment there was silence separating the space between us. And then everything changed.

"W-what are you doing?" I asked in shock, watching her dress hit the floor. The cotton material hadn't made a sound against the plush carpet, but I would've sworn that it was heard all around the Horn of Africa. Never before had I looked at Fatima with even the slightest bit of lust in my heart, but at this moment everything in me was screaming deserved praise for her beauty.

"What are you doing?" I asked again, noticing how weak my voice was getting as she slowly approached me.

"You said I have you, and if you mean that, then you're prepared to take care of me. Right?"

"R-right, but that doesn't mean—"

"It *does* mean in this way too because there's no one else I can go to or give myself to. Who can I trust besides you, right now, Royal?" She asked, slowly, lifting my t-shirt over my head.

"Fatima, this isn't a good idea. I-I don't even have any c-c-condoms," I stammered, wishing I didn't feel my body responding so powerfully to her touch.

It wasn't that I didn't want to do this, but I didn't want this to take away from our friendship because I needed that more than anything.

"We don't need a condom, you can just pull out before you cum," she said, unbuttoning my shorts, and pulling them down along with my boxers.

I thought I had one more protest left in me, but on her way back up from pulling my shorts down, my dick somehow slipped in between her lips, and I was lost. I'd known Fatima long enough to know, she was not a hoe, but the skills her mouth possessed were unlike any I'd experienced in my brief sexual history. I had no idea how I was still standing upright because by the time she had me tapping the back of her throat my knees felt like Jello.

"F-Fatima," I moaned, reaching for her head only to have her push my hands away, and push me back on the bed.

"I'm not gonna let you cum until I'm ready," she said, climbing on top of me.

Even though I wasn't too experienced at sex I knew that finishing before the female did was all the way bad, so I normally thought about anything other than what was going on in order to last longer. The moment, Fatima introduced my dick into her hot, wet, tight pussy, I knew that trick wouldn't work this time.

"Fatima, I c-can't," I whispered, trying to remember how to breathe.

"Just relax and let me do all the work."

She didn't move for a full thirty seconds, and when she did it was slow enough to make drying paint jealous. The only way to describe what I was feeling was to say it hurt so good that I never wanted it to end. She kept that slow and steady pace for a long five minutes before suddenly riding me hard and fast for the best minute of my life. I was so sure of reaching my looming climax that I was already basking in the after-glow in my mind, but she stopped when it was just out of reach.

"Wh-what—"

"Shhh, I know what I'm doing," she whispered against my lips.

I lost track of time after that, but when she finally let me cum pulling out of her was beyond impossible. I was so exhausted mentally and physically, I didn't even feel her climb off me before sleep became my new best friend. So, potent was her pussy power, that I actually dreamed of her, but in my dream, it was I who was making her a slave to my dick game. When I awoke it was with disappointment at being snatched away from the magical place where Fatima and I were one. I quickly took comfort in the fact that I could make my dreams a reality.

When I opened my eyes, I didn't find her in the bed next to me, and that's when I got a strange feeling. Something in my subconscious told me I hadn't simply awoken, something had awakened me. I got out of bed and pulled my shorts back on, noticing the purple sky outside my hotel window signaling nights final descent. I went into the living room expecting to find B.J. and Prince in front of the T.V., but the room was empty and dark. A quick check of Fatima's room yielded the same results and had me running back to my room for my pistol.

Fatima could've simply taken the boys out for a little while, but my instincts were screaming something different. Holding the gun in hand, I rushed to the front door, pulled it open, and stepped into the hall. I expected to see some guys from the security team posted up, but instead I saw two bodies slumped against the wall sporting fresh bullet holes still oozing blood and brain matter.

"Royal!" B.J. yelled.

As my head immediately snapped to the right I realized it was B.J. calling my name that had woke me up. Now I knew why. At the end of the hall holding the elevator door open was my oldest sister, looking the same as the last time I saw her. Only angrier. A few feet away from her stood Fatima holding Prince in her arms and holding onto B.J.'s hand, her eyes focused on me and they were wide with terror.

"Royal!" B.J. yelled again, jerking away from Fatima and making a mad dash towards me.

At that moment, everything started happening in slow motion. My focus shifted from the determination on B.J.'s face as his little legs moved with piston speed, to the mask of fear that had become Fatima's only expression. Maybe it was her maternal instinct that made her toss Prince to Free like a sack of potatoes so she could run after B.J., but as I raised my gun, I realized I didn't care. She betrayed me, and now she had to pay for that. I saw Free put Prince down inside the elevator and step back into the hall with her gun leveled in my direction, but I had the advantage, and I used it.

My first shot hit Fatima in the chest hard enough to bounce her off a wall and turn her around. My second shot tore through the back of her neck, sending her head first onto the floor. As an added bonus, I got to see that same bullet hit Free in the shoulder and knock her off her feet backward through the elevator door. By the time the elevator singed signaling it was going down B.J. had taken the final step needed to bring him close enough to leap into my arms.

"I got you, buddy," I said, catching him and quickly disappearing back inside our hotel room.

"Prince, get Prince," B.J. insisted, pointing towards the closed door.

I wanted to do exactly that, but I knew that might not be possible anymore. There was no way Free was alone, which meant we had to move *fast*. I ran straight to my room, sat B.J. on the bed and grabbed my phone. My first call was to alert the men I'd hired that two of their men were dead, and I was under attack. I received assurances that a car would be waiting in the garage, and I needed to get down there immediately. I put my shoes on, threw my laptop in the briefcase the diamonds were in, put B.J. on my back, and headed for the door.

"Hold on tight," I said.

"Prince, we coming to get you!" B.J. yelled, laughing.

Even in all this chaos, he had no idea what was going on, and I was thankful for that. His life and innocence were my responsibility. After opening the door slow I moved out into the hallway cautiously, heading for the stairs that were on the opposite direction of the elevator. The elevator would've been faster, but B.J. would've seen Fatima's lifeless body, and I didn't want that for him, or me.

Chapter 12
~Freedom~

It's-it's okay, Prince," I said, trying to soothe the screaming toddler while fumbling to pull my phone from my pocket.

The pain in my shoulder defied words, but it was no match for the pain in my heart. The fact that my own son, the baby boy I'd breathed life into, hadn't recognized me was devastating on a level that made me want to wail as loudly as Prince was. I knew I couldn't give in to that temptation though, I could still get B.J. back, but I needed help. Fighting through the pain I finally got my phone out and called Bone.

"I'm-I'm hit, meet me in the lobby," I said, hanging up and wishing the fucking elevator would go faster.

"Come here, Prince," I said gently, using my right hand to move the gun out of his sight while motioning him to me with my good arm.

He continued crying but came to me and took my hand. I didn't know how many hired gunmen Royal had at his disposal or what to expect when I reached the lobby, so I kept my gun out and concealed behind my back. When the elevator door finally slid open I was relieved to see Bone, Big Baby, and Destiny waiting on me.

"Are you okay?" Bone asked immediately, his eyes going straight to my shoulder.

"Yeah, the bullet went straight through. Destiny take Prince and get out of here, we've gotta find, Royal, before he goes away," I said.

"We'll find him, you need to go with your sister," Bone replied.

"No, I need to find our son," I said forcefully handing Prince off to Destiny and stepping back inside the elevator to cease all argument on what my next move would be.

I was just about to hit the button to return to the eighth floor when I spotted the cops rushing into the hotel, guns out and moving fast.

"Oh shit," I mumbled, trying to think fast.

"What? What is—"

"Don't turn around, it's the cops. Destiny walk away slowly. Bone you and Big Baby have gotta find Royal and B.J. The last time I saw him he was on the eighth floor, room eight-o-four. Hurry," I said, pushing my gun at him and quickly switching places with them so they could take the elevator.

"What are you about to do?" Bone asked, worriedly.

"I got this, just come find me at the local hospital," I replied, backing away from the elevator and falling to the floor.

"Miss are you okay?" A cop yelled, appearing at my side within seconds.

"I got-I got shot. Help me," I replied, in a hoarse whisper, forcing my eyelids down until they were barely open.

"We need medics and an ambulance quick!" The cop yelled to someone I couldn't see.

What I *did* see was the elevator door close, and I knew all I could do was pray that Bone and Big Baby got to my son in time. I didn't have to focus on my acting job because with each passing second the pain in my shoulder became more reality rap than NWA's first album. I was moments away from asking the cop hovering over me what the fucking hold up was when I heard the lobby around me come alive with radio chatter announcing the arrival of the ambulance.

"Just hold on Miss, the paramedics are here. Can you tell me who did this to you?" The cop asked.

Since I wasn't sure how I was gonna play my hand yet when it came to this line of questioning I simply moaned in pain. A stretcher skidding to a stop next to me prevented the cop from asking his question twice, and suddenly I was being lifted onto it and whisked away. Once I was in the back of the ambulance and we were on the move questions of a health nature were fired at me, and I was kept conscious with medication and constant reassurances that I'd be alright.

It was hard not to call the paramedics liars because I knew that the only way I would be alright was if I got my son back safely. Going into this situation, I hadn't thought Royal would harm a hair on B.J.'s head, but I'd witnessed the way he'd gunned Fatima down in that hallway, from the moment she'd made contact after receiving the video of her father's last moments she'd assured me she could get the kids to me by deceiving Royal. She said he'd never suspect it, and he'd never hurt her because he loved her like a sister.

She was right, but in the worse possible way, and I'd seen more than just the hurt of betrayal in his eyes when he'd dropped the hammer on Fatima. I'd seen his desperation, and that made him both unstable and unpredictable. A tiny piece of me hadn't wanted to kill him, but after my most recent encounter, I was quickly coming around to the fact, that I'd probably have to. I didn't know how to reason with him because it was clear his grief and hurt over what was done to our mother had corrupted his rational thinking.

He could've easily given both kids to me, the fact that he chose to shoot it out instead told me how far gone he was. All I could do right now was pray he didn't go over the edge any further. At least for my son's sake. The paramedics got me to the hospital within ten minutes, and I was immediately taken into surgery to get sewn up. Despite wanting to stay clear-headed, so I could strategize what to do next, I was more than thankful for the Morphine they doped me up with. By the time my back hit the operating room table, I was feeling nothing that resembled pain, and that allowed me to drift off to a long high above the clouds.

Aryanna

I had no idea how long it was before I came back down,
but when I did I found myself in a hospital room by myself,
handcuffed to the bed. It took me a few moments to clear the
screams of panic from my mind, and when I did, I immediately pulled my phone from my pocket. Not surprisingly, I
had a bunch of missed calls from everyone, but Bone was
the first person I called.

"Bone," I said, weakly.

"Thank God," he replied, with obvious relief filling his
voice.

"Why aren't you here?" I asked.

"I tried to see you, but the police won't let that happen
until they have your statement. They have no idea what happened, so they don't know if you're friend or foe, right now."

"I'm handcuffed to the bed," I said slowly.

"Oh shit, okay, don't worry because we're coming to you
and—"

"Do you have B.J.?" I asked.

His immediate silence was all the answer I needed, and I
could feel my heart break a little more.

"We'll get him back free, I promise."

I could already feel the tears in my throat, and if it hadn't
been for the tall, brown-skinned man, with long dreads coming into my room, I might've had a good cry with my husband on the phone. I knew that was impossible now though
because I could smell cop in any country.

"Wait for my call," I whispered, hanging up and
smoothly shutting off my phone before putting it back in my
pocket.

"Sorry to interrupt, but I have a few questions for you if
you feel up to talking," the cop said, taking a seat in the one
chair that sat by the rooms single window. Given my
lifestyle, I had a natural aversion to any law enforcement and
the conversations they liked to have, but this wasn't the U.S,
where there were rights to stand on or procedures to hide

behind. Righteous indignation wouldn't get me anything except more trouble.

"Who are you?" I asked.

"My name is Motiru, and I'm investigating what took place tonight at the Hotel Avalon. Can you tell me what happened?"

"I was shot," I replied, shortly.

"Yes, you were, and so were three other people, making it a total of four victims. Two different guns though, and you're the only survivor, so I would appreciate if you could walk me through what happened."

Telling the truth in any situation including the cops was a dangerous game because most of the time it was too crazy to be believable, and the benefit of the doubt was rarely given. However, lying in a way that was easily transparent could be an even bigger risk because nothing said would actually help. I wanted to say that I had no idea what had happened, but it was evident I'd been on the eighth floor and had to have seen those other people die. That meant the only card, I could play was the one of truth. At least mostly true.

"I came here to get my son and little brother back. They were kidnapped eighteen months ago, and I got a tip that they were here, so I showed up," I said.

"Kidnapped by who? And who tipped you off to their location?"

"That's a long story," I replied, tiredly.

"Why don't you just give me the highlights, Ms. Walker."

The fact that he knew my name had my heart jackhammering in my chest, but I kept my face exactly the same, and my eye contact remained direct.

"If you know my name then you know enough to put the pieces together without my assistance. Find my son," I demanded.

"We're looking for your son and your brothers, but due to some sophisticated tampering with the hotel's security system, we have no footage of them leaving. You wouldn't know anything about that, would you?"

"No, I didn't kill anybody."

"So, it was your thirteen-year-old brother, Royal?" He asked, skeptically.

"I could see how you might have a hard time believing that, but you seem well informed enough to know what, Royal, is capable of."

"Probably the same thing everyone with the last name Walker is capable of," he replied seriously.

"It's counterproductive to insult me, and I'm feeling weak from my surgery, so I would like to rest now," I said.

"I understand, but I would appreciate if you'd stay around. At least until we clear you of any wrongdoing with regards to this shooting, or the United States informs us of what they would like done with you," he replied, standing up.

"So, I'm under arrest?"

"Not yet, but you are in custody which is why I've loaned you one of my favorite pair of handcuffs. Before I forget, I'm gonna need your phone," he said, holding his hand out expectantly.

Cutting me off from the world outside right now had me feeling more anxious than I could ever remember being. I fought not to show it as I dug my phone back out of my pocket. I wasn't worried about anyone having access to the contents of my phone because the moment someone tried to crack my password the phone would cannabinol itself. I just didn't want to feel alone and vulnerable right now.

"So, what happens when I need to make a call," I asked, reluctantly handing my phone over.

"You'll just have to wait until you get to the jail, but don't you worry because the doctor should clear you for transfer within the next forty-eight hours. Sleep tight," he said, smiling as he left the room.

The Boss Man's Daughters 5

I was wishing for my gun at this moment, so I could've blown the smirk off his face, but since that wasn't possible I hit the button on my morphine drip until sleep begged me to come home. Despite the good dope navigating its way through my system, my sleep was still restless, especially when I tried to roll over and my arm didn't cooperate. Somehow, I managed to rest beyond the rising of the sun, only waking up when a nurse came in and brought me a plate of food.

I didn't realize how hungry I was until I saw the plate sitting on the rolling table in front of me. The pains in my stomach were enough to have me wiping away my eye buggers with a quickness while hitting the buttons to raise the bed, so I could get to it on some fat girl shit. Whatever it was smelled delicious, but when I pulled the lid up I couldn't identify one thing on the plate. Part of me thought it was gonna start moving on its own!

"I can't wait to see what the jail food is like," I said aloud, covering the plate back up in frustration.

"Hopefully, you'll never have to find out," a woman said, from the doorway of my room.

I looked up to see a white woman that I didn't know, but by the way, she was dressed, I knew who she was here representing.

"I think you've got the wrong room," I said.

"I doubt that Freedom, but if you need another moment to yourself I can come back."

"Who are you and what do you want?" I asked, not the least bit interested in playing games with this bitch.

"My name is Madeline, and I'm here at the behest of a mutual friend."

"I don't have any friends in the army," I replied, looking her up and down in her pressed dress uniform.

"It's actually the Marines, but honestly I don't have too many friends there anymore either," she said, coming all the way into the room and closing the door behind her.

"You could've fooled me."

"I'll tell you a secret, I'm actually a newly retired general, but for the purposes of this visit I'm still active," she whispered, smiling.

"Okay, so what's the purpose of this visit, to take me back to the United States to stand trial for my crimes?"

"You and I both know that you wouldn't get a fair trial. Maybe a fair *execution*, but never a fair trial," she replied, shaking her head.

I didn't say anything, I just looked at this goofy bitch until she finally decided to *make* her fucking point before I lost my patience.

"Yeah, he warned me that you weren't one for small talk. I'm here to get you out of this situation," she said.

"And how do you plan to do that?"

Before she could answer, the door to my room was opened and in walked the same cop from last night.

"Ah, Mr. Motiru, I'm so glad you could come on such short notice. I trust everything is in order," Madeline said, smiling.

I could tell by the look on his face that he liked her as much as I did, but whatever was going on he liked even less. He didn't utter a word, he simply walked over to my bed, uncuffed me, handed me my phone, and left the room as quickly as he'd come.

"What the fuck just happened?" I asked, in disbelief.

"Well, we can stay here while I waste time explaining, or we can get the fuck out of here."

The decision wasn't a difficult one for me to make, and I began unhooking my I.V line immediately. When my feet hit the floor, I was unsteady for a second, but I shook it off and followed Madeline's lead. I kept waiting for someone to step out and put the bracelets back on me, but it never happened, and we made it out front to a waiting black Chevy Tahoe. We climbed in and Madeline wasted no time getting away from there.

"I appreciate you getting me out of that situation, however, you managed to pull it off, but you can take me to the marina. It's best to put Jamaica in my rearview," I said.

"I couldn't agree more, but before you do that there's a stop we need to make first. It'll go a long way towards answering your questions, and don't worry because the paperwork that got you out is official so they can't change their mind."

Part of me was thinking this bitch had *lost* her mind, and I better tuck and roll the next time this truck came to a stop. The only thing that prevented me from doing it was the need I had to know what wizard was behind the curtain pulling strings for me. Whoever it was had juice because this woman representing the same government that wanted to crucify me, had somehow just secured my life back. That took more than money, so I rode on in silence. Twenty minutes later, we arrived at the same hotel I'd just been shot in.

"You're fucking with me, right!" I asked, looking at her like the crazy person she obviously was.

"Don't worry, we're on the second floor, not the eighth. Come on," she said, getting out of the SUV.

To say I was reluctant was an understatement, but I got out anyway and followed her inside. I felt like every pair of eyes was on us, but I knew that was simply paranoia trying to take over. Still, I was grateful when we finally got to room two-o-seven, and I was safely behind a closed door.

"So, where is this mystery person who supposedly sent you? I'm assuming that's why we're here," I said, following her further into the suite.

When she didn't answer I thought she was ignoring me, and that pissed me off.

"Look, bitch, I don't got time for games so—"

Suddenly my voice refused to work as the figure sitting on the bed came into clear view. The four-inch-thick beard and the dreadlocks had severely altered his appearance, but I'd still know that face anywhere.

"Come touch me and see if I'm real," he challenged.

The sound of his voice made me close my eyes, but the tears fell anyway.

"You c-can't be real, you died in my arms. Daddy, you died in my arms."

Chapter 13
~Angel~

"Any word from, Free, yet?" I asked Bone, joining him at the dining room table.

"Nothing, and it's driving me batshit crazy! I swear, I'm gonna tie her ass up somewhere on this boat, and never let her out of my fucking sight once she gets back!"

"I didn't know my sister was into the kinky shit, but that's y'all business," I replied, hoping to lighten the mood.

He didn't so much as crack a smile, I knew I had to switch tactics.

"From what you told me she played the situation smart which gave you a fighting chance to get to Royal and B.J.," I said.

"No, she played the situation dumb by being hardheaded and insisting on going to meet up with Fatima by herself, instead of all of us going.

She only played the aftermath smart, and we see how far that got us. Royal and my son are in the fucking wind, and my wife is handcuffed to a hospital bed in a country that's more than a little friendly with the United States government."

I couldn't argue that the situation wasn't a fucked up one, but we'd definitely been in worse and managed to survive. We just had to pray that we had more lives than an alley cat.

"How's Kamile?" Destiny asked, coming into the dining room, followed closely by Big Baby.

"She's fine, downstairs sleeping," I replied.

"What about Prince?" Destiny asked.

"Sleeping right next to her and hasn't left her side except to use the bathroom. I've always wondered how young kids are when they start to develop memories because I *swear* that little boy remembered his momma. He's so calm and comfortable around her," I replied.

"He definitely wasn't that when Free gave him to me, but I guess that's understandable given what he must've witnessed," Destiny said.

"That ain't no lie. Speaking of kids, where the rest of our heathens?" I asked.

"The last time I checked they were playing in Free's cabin and Lil' Boy was going to check on them," Destiny replied.

I felt guilty that I'd spent almost no time with my son in recent memory, but I felt like I owed it to Kamile to be by her side until she was better. I knew what it felt like to be confined to a bed while the world still moved around you. Even though Kamile wasn't in the same situation I had been in, I still needed her to know she was still a part of everyday life. Times were tough, and the struggle was getting real every day. But, the moment of joy and tears I got to share with her as I watched her reunite with her son made it all worth it.

I wanted to spend time with my own son, but I had to remain focused, so I could give Free the same joy and peace that Kamile had.

"Any word on Royal and B.J.?" I asked.

"No, that little bastard adapts and blends like a chameleon. The two dead mufuckas that Free must've shot worked for a private security firm based out of Europe, and it stands to reason that they're the ones helping Royal, right now. Because of that, I have no idea if he's even still in Jamaica," Bone replied, clearly frustrated.

"We've gotta figure out some way to draw him out," Destiny said.

"He's gotta be running out of places to hide, and the U.S. is only gonna step up the intensity to find him once Jamaican authorities report what's happened," Bone stated.

"What makes you think they'll report it?" I asked.

"The same thing that makes me believe they didn't hand-cuff Free to her hospital bed, simply because they had unanswered questions about her involvement in what happened at the hotel. I think they know who Free *really* is, which makes her a big fish to catch in this little ass pond," Bone replied.

"How would they know that?" Destiny asked.

No one gave a verbal answer, but the looks we exchanged said we were all drawing the same conclusions. It had to have been Royal.

"So, while they should be focusing on Royal and B.J. they're probably only worried about, Free," I said, shaking my head.

"That's that bullshit, and we gotta do something about it," Destiny said, looking at Big Baby.

"I know that look Destiny Walker," I said.

"Go get her," Bone said, agreeing without having to be asked.

"Go get who?" Lil' Boy asked, coming into the room.

"Free, and you're coming with us," Destiny replied, pushing him back through the doorway.

"Don't even *think* your ass is leaving me here with the kids and Kamile," Bone said, stopping my standing motion before I could get fully upright.

"But—"

"But my ass, it ain't happening so let's focus on what the next move needs to be once they get back with, Free," Bone demanded.

I wanted to go help the others, but the look on Bone's face told me, I'd be wasting my breath trying to reason with him. So, I sat my ass back down.

"Well, obviously once we've got Free we've gotta get *far* the fuck away from here, but the question is where do we go next," I said.

"I've got somewhat of an idea about that, but shit might get ugly."

"How is that different from any other adventure we embark on?" I asked, seriously.

"True. Well, we've gotta find out where Royal is, and I only see one way to do that. The security company he hired has to know the location of their employees at all times, so I figured we'd ask them."

"And by ask, you mean—" I said, knowing exactly what he meant.

"There's only one way any of us know how to ask questions and if ever there was a situation that required guerilla tactics this is it."

"Agreed. Once we've got Free and we're on the move, we can contact our people to find out everything we can about whoever runs the security company. What happens if we corner Royal and he gives up B.J. without a fight?" I asked.

"To be honest with you, I don't know. Even though, Free agreed to go after, Royal. I think she was secretly hoping not to kill him, but now he's shot her *and* took off with our son, again. The safe bet is he's already a dead man, and he's gonna die by your sister's hand," he replied, truthfully.

There was no joy in his declaration, and there was none in my heart, as I acknowledged the probability that he was right. I couldn't excuse Royal of any wrongdoing for the decisions he'd made, but I couldn't completely put everything on him either. It all started with Sapphire and her betrayal, and now here we were. Somehow, even with that bitch in the ground, she was still wreaking havoc on the children she never should've been blessed to have. Hate wasn't a strong enough word for what I felt for her.

"It's times like this when I wish my dad was still alive," I said, softly.

The look Bone gave me was a mixture of understanding and guilt, which made me feel bad for what I'd said. It was insensitive because I knew he still felt partially responsible for insisting that Free leave the country immediately, instead of after the situation with our mother was handled. I was told that Free and him had worked through that troubling time, but it was obvious Bone was still carrying a huge burden.

"I'm sorry, I didn't think before I said that," I confessed, lamely.

"You don't have to apologize, it should be me who—"

"Uh-uh, don't do that. I've known you a long time and I know, you would never do anything to intentionally hurt my sister. You're smart enough to know that you can't live life with shoulda, woulda, coulda's, so you have to accept what's happened and move on," I said, sincerely.

He nodded his head in understanding and gave me a smile of gratitude.

"Now that we have the foundation for our next move, I have a question about the immediate future. What do we do with Fatima's mom?" I asked, reluctantly.

The look he gave me said it all, but he made it crystal clear when he pulled a .380 pistol from his pocket and passed it to me.

"I thought you might say that," I replied, taking the gun and standing up.

I had no doubt that if shit had gone the way it was supposed to have gone Free would've let Fatima and her mom live, but now the woman downstairs was simply a liability. We didn't need that, and since I had nothing better to do, why not take care of the problem.

"We'll dump the body once we're back at sea," Bone called after me.

I made my way back downstairs with the intention of handling the business real quick, but the sounds of children playing forced me to tuck the gun into the pocket of my jeans, and check on them. I tried to open the door quietly, but God's head whipped around, and as soon as he saw me he ran straight towards me.

"Mommy!" He screamed, smiling like I was his favorite person in the world, and opening his arms wide.

I immediately scooped him up in my arms and held him tight, inhaling his little kid smell until it was tickling the back of my throat and embedded in my brain.

"Hey, little man, what you doing?" I asked.

"I playing," he replied, enthusiastically.

I could see Faith playing with a pile of toys, and Grace was laying on her back in her crib just kicking her tiny legs with unexplained joy. Inside these walls, they were oblivious to the world around them and I truly loved that. All of us in this family was far from perfect but making sure our kids had the best lives possible was what we needed to pardon us of our sins in the end. I got right down on the floor next to Faith and immersed myself in the world of make-believe with my son, until my phone started going off, interrupting us. I ignored it for the first eight rings, but when the silence only lasted a full ten seconds before it started ringing again I reluctantly pulled myself away from the kids to answer it.

"What's up, Dee?" I asked, by way of answering.

"Freedom is not in the hospital or at the local jail, and I'm freaking the fuck out because nobody will tell us anything."

"Okay, just calm down, and tell me what happened," I replied, trying to soothe her.

"We showed up to do our thing, but the room she'd spent the night in was empty, and none of the nurses knew when she'd left because they still had her in the system. So, we figured they must've taken her to the jail and booked her, but when we got there, there's no record of her in the fucking system! I'm telling you, this feels *wrong* Angel and I'm about to panic," she warned.

"Panicking won't get us nowhere so just chill. There has to be a logical explanation because there's no way she could've been extradited that quick. It's not like, Free, wouldn't put up every legal fight possible to avoid extradition, and that shit takes time. She's still in Jamaica."

"But, *where* Angel?" Destiny asked, emotionally.

I could tell that my calmness was in no way rubbing off on her, and her fear was threatening to overtake her at any moment. I knew exactly how she felt because Free was the closest thing either of us had to an actual mother, and all we knew at the moment, was that she was somewhere unknown and hurt. Imagining anything about that scenario was absolutely terrifying.

"Where are you?" I asked.

"Down the street from the police station."

"Okay, come back to the boat so we can regroup and figure this shit out," I instructed.

"We're on our way."

I hung up trying to figure out what the fuck I was gonna tell Bone, as if having no idea where his son was in the world wasn't bad enough. When I looked up I saw him coming out of Kamile's room carrying a sleeping Prince, and I knew I'd better find the words fast.

"You might want to put him back because we've got a—why are you looking at me like that?" I asked, noticing the strange look in his eyes.

"Hold on," he replied, disappearing into my cabin, then reappearing without Prince.

"You could've left him sleep with his mom," I said, confused by his actions.

"No, I couldn't."

His words gave me a feeling I couldn't explain, and before I knew it my feet were moving on their own accord in the direction of Kamile's room. I didn't know what I'd expected to find when I peeked in on her, but I found her sleeping as peacefully as when I'd left her a while ago. I turned to Bone even more confused, but his grave expression hadn't changed. I looked back in on Kamile, preparing to go to her, and that's when I saw it. Her chest wasn't moving. She wasn't breathing.

Aryanna

Chapter 14
~Destiny~

"What did Angel say?" Lil' Boy asked.

"She said, we need to go back to the boat, so we can put our heads together and figure this shit out."

"Is she gonna tell, Bone?"

"I didn't ask, but I know damn well, *I'm* not trying to be the one to deliver that news," I replied, shaking my head.

"I know what you mean. The last time Free went missing, I thought Bone would lose his mind, but B.J. made that impossible because he had to stay focused for his son. Now both of them are missing," Lil' Boy said sadly.

"Stating the obvious *ain't* helping, my nigga. We need to find my sister or burn this whole fucking country to the ground."

Big Baby put his hand on my shoulder briefly to calm me down, then he pulled his phone out. When I read the text, I nodded my head in approval before turning back to Lil' Boy.

"Your brother thinks we need to find out who the cop was assigned to investigate the shooting at the hotel last night. Then we'll get answers from him," I said.

"That means I have to go *back* inside the police station," Lil' Boy replied, with displeasure.

We just looked at him expectantly, because with one female with the last name Walker already missing it damn sure wasn't smart for me to make that type of appearance. Lil' Boy huffed in frustration but headed back up the block in the direction we'd come a short while ago. The police station was only about a clock and a half away, so we saw him until he disappeared inside the building. Despite my best efforts to fight off the bad feelings I had about Free's whereabouts, I could still feel anxiety building in me, making me feel like

I was gonna be sick. Big Baby's text about getting something to eat from the carryout spot we were standing in front of didn't help either.

"I'm not hungry," I said.

He didn't argue by sending me another text, he stared me down until I gave in and went to the window to order. I ordered curry chicken for both of us and we took seats at a table set up on the sidewalk. I truly wasn't hungry, but I didn't need this nigga on my back about not taking care of myself, so I ate. By the time we finished our food ten minutes later, Lil' Boy still wasn't back, and my anxiety was approaching next level. I was just about to text Big Baby about him going down to check the situation out when I spotted Lil' Boy's lanky frame headed in our direction.

"There he is," I said, pointing.

I could tell by the pace of his stride that he'd found something out, and by the time he reached our table, I was already on my feet.

"Well?" I asked, impatiently.

"The investigator we want to talk to is a guy named Motiru, but he's not in, right now."

"Where the fuck is he?" I asked, more than a little frustrated.

"He's right here," a voice said, from my left.

I looked over to see a slender, built, brown-skinned man with long dreads sitting at a table a few feet away, chewing his food thoughtfully while evaluating us carefully.

"You're Motiru," I said.

"Yeah, I am, but I don't know any of you," he replied, moving the pistol he'd been concealing under the table into plain view with deliberate slowness.

"My last name is Walker, so you should know that your gun doesn't faze me at all, plus these two gentlemen here will make sure you join me in hell. Besides I just want to talk to you," I stated, calmly.

I could tell by the flicker in his eyes that my name meant something to him, which only confirmed that Lil' Boy had the right information. The only thing we could do now was hope this cop knew how to make good decisions.

"What do we have to talk about?" Motiru asked.

"My sister, I need to know where she is," I replied.

"How the hell should I know?" He said, angrily.

"Because you were the one leading the investigation into last night's shooting, and you insisted on being the only one to interview her in the hospital. She's not at the hospital or the jail so, where is she?" Lil' Boy asked, with barely controlled fury.

"Like I said, how the hell should I know? Once I took the handcuffs off her she was no longer my responsibility," Motiru replied, in the same angry tone.

"Wait, are you saying you *released* her, as in she's no longer in your custody?" I asked, confused.

"Welcome to the party, Ms. Walker," Motiru said, with heavy sarcasm.

Big Baby took a step towards him, but I grabbed his arm and shook my head because we didn't have time for that.

"What you're saying doesn't make sense, if my sister was out I'd be one of the first people to know it," I said, patiently.

"I never said that Freedom Walker was *free*, I just said she was no longer in *my* custody," Motiru replied, smiling.

His smile was quick, but Lil' Boy's draw was quicker, it was almost like the two-tone Glock .40 in his hand had materialized out of thin air.

"If you think we've got time to play games with you, then you've got us fucked up, and confused. If you think, I won't put a hole in your head, right here on this public street, in broad daylight, this close to the police station, you've got me fucked up *and* you're confused. Last time, I'm gonna ask you, where-the fuck-is, Freedom Walker?" Lil' Boy's tone was cold and calm.

Aryanna

To my amazement, the people around us weren't panicked in the slightest like it was an everyday occurrence for two mufuckas to be waving guns in public. Part of me thought this cop would continue to take us for a joke but watching him look closely at Lil' Boy told me that he knew better.

"A United States Marine showed up with paperwork stating that Freedom Walker, was to be released into her custody for transport back to the United States," Motiru stated.

"Your lying," I replied quickly, despite the horrible feeling I was getting in the pit of my stomach.

"Why would I lie," Motiru countered, tucking his gun into his pants.

"The U.S. can't extradite that fast, there's court proceeding that has to take place first," I argued.

"I thought so, too, but the paperwork listed your sister as being wanted under the patriot act for domestic terrorism. Terrorists don't have rights," Motiru replied, smirking.

Everything in me wanted to knock the smirk off this nigga's face, but I kept my cool.

"This general, what was her name?" Lil' Boy asked.

"Madeline Parker. That's all I know, and I suggest you all leave now before I contact her to pick up this Walker bitch, too," Motiru replied, dismissively.

I didn't know what I planned to say when I opened my mouth, but before I had the chance to formulate the words Big Baby pulled his gun and shot the cop between his eyes. The people around us may have been comfortable seeing guns, but when that shot rang out everybody scattered quick. We simply walked away, slid into our stolen Nissan Maxima and blended with traffic.

"Your ass is crazy," Lil' Boy said, looking at Big Baby in the rearview mirror. Big Baby immediately fired a text to my phone that I read out loud.

"We don't tolerate disrespect, especially towards our women."

Lil' Boy wasn't about to argue with that, because he would've done the same thing involving, Angel. The problem now was that Big Baby's action would only add more heat to our situation, making it impossible to stay in Jamaica and pick up the trail of this general who had Free.

"Where would they be taking her?" I asked, aloud.

"I don't know, but if they're treating her like a terrorist, they're gonna throw her in the darkest hole they can find," Lil' Boy replied.

"We can't let that happen," I said, firmly.

"Agreed, but how do we stop it?" Lil' Boy asked.

"Just drive and let me think," I replied, feeling my anxiety steadily increasing with each passing second.

I needed to talk to Angel, but just as I was about to call her my phone started ringing. Looking at the name of the caller made my heart stop in my chest.

"Free, are you okay?" I asked, immediately.

"I'm fine, I'm fine. Where are you?" She asked.

"Still in Jamaica, but we're about to get on the move a.s.a.p and—"

"No, we can't leave yet," she replied, quickly.

"We, you mean, you're still here? The cop just told us that some Marine bitch came and got you, to take you back to the U.S.," I said, looking over at Lil' Boy.

"I'll explain everything when you get here."

"Where the fuck are you?" I asked, confused and frustrated.

"I'm at the hotel Avalon, Room two-o-seven. How long will it take you to get here?" she asked.

"Bitch what? You're at the hotel where you got shot? Why would you—"

"Stay focused, Destiny. How long will it take you to get here?" Free asked again.

"I don't know, am I supposed to go get Angel and-"

"No, we won't be here long. Just hurry up," she replied, disconnecting before I could say anything else.

"Remind me to beat that bitch up when I see her," I said, still looking at my phone.

"Is she really at the hotel Avalon?" Lil' Boy asked, in disbelief.

"I guess we'll find out when we get there," I replied, feeling relief through my frustration.

I got a text from the back seat asking me the same thing, I knew his brother was probably thinking.

"No, it's probably not a smart move to stick around after you just knocked off a cop, but do you think it's a good idea to leave, Free, in Jamaica?" I asked, turning around in my seat to look at Big Baby.

I could tell by the look on his face that my point had been made. We rode on in silence, arriving at the hotel fifteen minutes later.

"Let's go," I said, checking my snub nose .45 to make sure it was ready, as I got out of the car.

I led the way through the lobby, choosing to take the stairs instead of the elevator, bringing us to room 207 without incident. I tapped on the door, making sure to look up and down the hall for any signs of a threat or law enforcement. I knew Free would never set us up, but that didn't mean we hadn't been followed from the carryout. When the door was pulled open, I was expecting Free or even the Marine bitch, but what I saw had me in shock, then I was falling.

Chapter 15
~Father-God~

"Nice catch bring her inside, and lay her on the bed," I instructed Big Baby stepping aside allowing everyone entry.

I could tell him and his brother was surprised to see me alive, too, but their pride wouldn't allow them to faint like my youngest daughter had. After closing the door behind them, I followed their lead further into the room, noticing how Big Baby didn't lay Destiny on the bed but instead sat on the bed with her still cradled in his arms.

"How is this possible?" Lil' Boy asked, looking at me like the ghost he thought I was.

"That's a long story, and if it's all the same to you, I'd rather tell it to everyone at once," I replied.

"Trust me, as unbelievable as the shit is gonna sound it all makes sense," Free said.

"Okay, so is she friend or foe?" Lil' Boy asked, nodding towards Madeline.

"She's with me," I said, in a tone that left no room for argument.

I watched Lil' Boy, Big Baby, and Free exchange looks, reminding me of the time we'd all spent together in Chicago before all hell broke loose. Their loyalty to my daughter was unparalleled. I knew they'd follow Free's orders before mine, no matter how dangerous they knew I was. When Free gave the nod, I saw them visibly relax.

"So, why did you want us to meet you here?" Lil' Boy asked Free.

"Because if there's any chance, Royal is still in Jamaica with B.J., I wanna hit the ground running, and don't worry I'm not in jeopardy of being rearrested," Free replied.

"I don't know if, Royal is still around, but I doubt it. He's hired a security firm to guard him and the smart move would be to get him out of town quickly and quietly. Either way though, it's not a good idea to stay here," Lil' Boy said.

"Why is that?" I asked, seeing something in his eyes that hinted trouble could be lurking.

"We had a little run-in with the police," Lil' Boy replied vaguely.

"By run-in, you mean what?" Free asked.

Lil' Boy looked at his brother, then both of them looked at Madeline before their eyes rested on, Free. The message of mistrust was clear, and it was starting to piss me off.

"I said, she's-with-me," I repeated, in a low growl, looking squarely at both men.

"Dad, I got this, Lil' Boy you can speak freely. Madeline is family now," Free said, looking at her.

Despite how much I'd told Madeline about Free, she couldn't yet understand how big of a deal it was to have earned her respect and loyalty. She would soon see, though.

"Basically, the cop that tried to arrest you threatened, Destiny and called her a bitch, so Big Baby shot him in the head," Lil' Boy stated, calmly.

When I looked at Big Baby I could tell he'd make the same decision a hundred times over, and that made me smile inside.

"When and where did this happen?" I asked.

"Not even a half an hour ago, about a block from the police station," Lil' Boy replied.

"You shot a cop—in broad daylight?" Free asked, clearly annoyed.

Big baby just looked at her, his stare unflinching even though he knew she was obviously upset.

"We need to get on the move," I said, nodding towards Madeline to help me pack our shit so we could go.

"Was he serious?" Madeline whispered to me, as we grabbed the one duffle bag we'd been living out of. I didn't answer until we were in the bathroom collecting our toiletries.

"Sweetheart, nobody in that room is the type to lie about a homicide just to have interesting dinner conversation, so if he said it, it's true," I said.

"Oh," she replied softly.

I could tell by the look on her face, that she was trying to come to terms with her new reality, and it made me feel bad.

"I've got an idea, why don't you go up to your house in Maine, I'll meet you once everything is sorted out," I offered.

"Or you could come with me now."

"Baby, I'd love to, but we set this plan of escape in motion to keep my kids from killing each other."

"*And* to give us our happily ever after," she countered.

"You're right, but you know what has to happen first. That doesn't mean, you have to be with me for whatever comes next. I would feel better if I knew you were somewhere safe."

"I'd feel better knowing the same thing about you Jon, but you're preparing to wade into the middle of this storm and there's no way I'm letting you do that alone. End of discussion," she replied.

I'd known her long enough to know that arguing at this point was nothing more than a waste of time and energy, so I kissed her passionately instead.

"Good dick is not gonna make me change my mind," she said, once I'd pulled our lips apart.

"How about *amazing* dick?"

"Very funny," she replied, putting the rest of our stuff into the bag and zipping it up. By the time we walked back into the bedroom, it was clear, Free had put her anger aside and had everyone ready to move.

"We're probably gonna drain some stares with you carrying Destiny, but we've gotta move like it's no big deal. We'll take the stairs to the lobby and once we get there, I'll be in front, Lil' Boy I want you on my left, to block as much of the front desks view as possible, and Big Baby you fall in directly behind me. Any questions?" I asked, looking around at everybody.

"What are you two driving?" Lil' Boy asked.

"An SUV, why?" Madeline replied.

"Because it's probably not a good idea to be riding around in a stolen car, especially since it's the same one that was at a recent crime scene," Lil' Boy said.

I could tell that Free was seconds away from giving those niggas another tongue lashing, but I held my hand up to stop her because we didn't have time for that shit.

"Let's move," I instructed, taking Madeline's hand, leading the way.

We made it downstairs to the truck without a problem, but the police presence, once we got on the road, had us all a little nervous. Apparently, Jamaica took cop killing as serious as any other country. Madeline kept her cool though and got us safely to the marina, but once we arrived my nervousness increased. I was moments away from walking head first into an unavoidable emotional situation. Not only would I be reunited with my daughter, but I was about to meet my son, Kamile and I had created, *and* Kamile, too.

Madeline knew almost everything about me and my family, but I'd never mentioned Kamile, and when she had I didn't know how to tell her that the second little boy Royal kidnapped was my son, too. I'd wanted to confess this secret to Madeline when Free told me, she'd managed to get Prince back, but I still couldn't find the words. The time for procrastination and bullshitting was over though because we were here now.

"You want me to go in first?" Free offered.

"No, baby, let's do this together," I replied, opening my door and stepping out.

Once we were all on the sidewalk Free took my hand and led the way. Behind me, I could hear Destiny stirring before I heard her voice.

The Boss Man's Daughters 5

"B-babe why are you carrying me?" She asked, groggy and confused.

I pulled Free to a stop and turned around, so Destiny could see me.

"Ho-ly shit! I wasn't dreaming, you're alive!" She yelled, hopping out of Big Baby's arms and into mine.

"Yes, baby Dee, I'm alive," I replied, rubbing her back soothingly as she sobbed with tears of joy.

I didn't anticipate an end anytime soon for the flood of tears she was letting loose, so I turned around and continued towards the yacht with her in my arms. When we were only a few feet away Bone stepped out onto the deck and Free flew to him in a dead run, knocking him off balance when she leaped into his arms. By the time I'd made it on board, they were on the ground laughing and kissing until he saw me.

"Impossible," Bone whispered, scrambling to his feet.

"Nothing is impossible for, Father-God," I replied, seriously.

Bone looked from me to Free, and back to me before shaking his head and smiling.

"How daddy, *how* are you alive?" Destiny asked, finally getting her emotions under control enough for her to talk.

"I'll explain it to you in a minute, but let's get Angel and Kamile together, too," I replied, setting her on her feet.

I noticed Bone's smile falter, and I didn't like the feeling it caused in me.

"What is it?" I asked, directing my question at Bone.

He didn't respond immediately but instead whispered something in Free's ear. The look she turned on me let me know that whatever he'd just told her was nothing good.

"Come on dad," Free said, taking me by the hand, leading me further inside the yacht.

Destiny quickly grabbed my other hand making it clear, she wasn't about to be left behind. We were led down a flight of stairs and to the door of one of the boats sleeping cabins.

"I'm so sorry, daddy," Free murmured, before pushing the door open.

I had no idea what she meant, but her words had my heart banging in my chest. I reluctantly followed her through the door and found Angel sitting next to a sleeping Kamile, holding her hand. I wasn't surprised to find Kamile still laid up after being shot, but the tears running down Angel's cheeks were a surprise, especially since they obviously came from a place of sorrow.

"Angel," I said, letting Free's and Destiny's hands go, and moving towards the bed.

"Oh my, God-d-dad is it really you," she replied, standing up and throwing herself into my open arms.

"It's me, sweetheart, it's me. Are you okay?" I asked, pulling back so I could look her in the eyes.

I could tell she waited to say something, but the wave of emotion pushing her under was too strong for words. I pulled her closer to me, knowing that my physical presence and support was better than any words I could offer anyway. Suddenly, I felt Free and Destiny wrapping their arms around us, and we all huddled together sharing tears. It wasn't until I looked over to see if our blubbering had woken Kamile that I noticed something strange. Her face was pale, and she was still. Too still.

"Kamile," I called out, trying to move towards her.

I was surprised when Angel and Free wouldn't let me go to her, but when I looked down at Angel I finally understood why.

"Wh-what happened?" I asked, looking at Kamile again.

"I don't know, Bone found her when he went to check on her. We thought she was healing fine from her gunshots, but apparently not," Angel replied, sadly.

My heart ached to know that Kamile was really gone. Despite my relationship with Madeline my love for Kamile had never died, and it hurt me that she would never know just how much she meant to me.

"Give me a minute with her. I'll meet you all back upstairs," I said, softly.

They all hugged me one more time before hovering my request. I made my way slowly to the bed and sat down next to her, taking her hand in mine.

"It's been a long time Ms. Armstrong, but you're still as beautiful as always. I've missed you. I heard we have a son, Prince Jonathan Walker. Thank you for that. I promise to take care of him and raise him in a way that will make you proud. I will *never* let him forget you or the amazing love that created him. I feel blessed to have shared time and space with you. Thank you for everything you ever did for me and my daughters. I'm so s-sorry this happened to you," I said, watching my teardrops fall on her hand as I kissed it.

I leaned over and kissed her softly on the lips one last time, wishing with all my heart she could somehow wrap her arms around me and kiss me back.

"I love you still and I promise to tell our son that every day for the rest of my life," I vowed.

After spending a couple more minutes starring at her and forever imprinting her face in my memory. I pulled myself together, kissed her on the forehead, and left the room. It took a few deep breaths before I felt emotionally stable enough to make my way back upstairs. I followed the chorus of voices until I found everyone seated around a dining room table. My arrival ceased all conversation and turned all eyes in my direction.

"I want a proper burial for her with a headstone, my son can visit one day," I said.

"Y-your son?" Madeline asked, with a puzzled expression.

"Kamile's son is my son, but that's a conversation we can have later," I replied.

"Where do you want her buried, dad?" Angel asked.

Aryanna

My first instinct was to suggest Chicago, but there was no way any of us could or should step foot back in the United States.

"Where do you think she would rest peacefully?" I asked.

"She was fond of Russia," Angel replied, thoughtfully.

"I want it done then, use whatever money you have," I demanded.

"Kamile put me in control of her money a while ago, and Angel was to be Prince's guardian," Free said.

"Okay. We lay her to rest before anything else, understand?" I asked, locking eyes with every person at the table to make sure there was no miscommunication.

No one spoke, but everyone nodded in agreement which meant I could move on to the next topic on everyone's mind.

"For the past two years, you all thought I was dead, and for all intents and purposes I was. I didn't die that night on that hotel room floor in Chicago. The paramedics were able to restart my heart long enough to get me into surgery. It was touch and go, but they managed to nurse me back to health, and once they were sure I wouldn't die they buried me in Guantanamo Bay."

"Cuba—they had you in, *Cuba*?" Angel asked, in disbelief.

"Yeah, and that's where they planned for me to spend the rest of my life. The world thought I was dead, and as long as the government could keep it that way they'd never have to explain how they let me rot in prison for killing a woman who was still alive. You all were able to force their hand the first time because you knew I was alive, and they hadn't sent me to Cuba or Colorado yet. With you all believing I was dead there was no one for you to look for," I replied.

"They went through all of that, for you?" Destiny asked,

"Your father is kind of a big deal in certain circles. Well, he *was*. Even if he hadn't been though the U.S. government will do *whatever* possible to keep their dirty little secrets buried, and it's been that way since they *'discovered'* America," Madeline said, using her fingers to make air quotations.

"And how exactly do you fit in?" Angel asked.

"He made me fall in love with him," Madeline replied, smiling at me.

Her declaration turned all eyes in my direction.

"Madeline worked intelligence for the Marines and she was stationed at Guantanamo. Of course, the government wasn't just content to let me rot, they wanted to pick my brain and see what I knew, but I wouldn't bend, break, or fold. I did feed Madeline just enough bullshit to require us to have weekly conversations," I said, smiling slightly.

"Yeah, well, I saw right through your bullshit," Madeline countered.

"You did, and I'm glad because that gave you a chance to see the real me. She played hard to get for a while, but we eventually became friends, then more. When I felt I could trust her, I had her start looking out for any information on you all, but nothing came up after the shit you all pulled in Tennessee breaking Angel out. Nice work by the way," I said, sincerely.

"Speaking of breakouts, how are you here now? Are you two on the run?" Angel asked.

"No, I'm retired and drawing full benefits courtesy of the United States Marine corps," Madeline stated, honestly.

"And I'm still a dead man," I replied, nonchalantly.

Except for Free and Madeline, everyone else's expressions were calling bullshit on our simplistic answers, meaning I needed to elaborate. "I was given drugs to make it appear like I was dead, and a death certificate was quickly issued, and filed by the government. They dated it of course to cover their asses, but it turns out they were covering mine, too," I confessed.

"We decided to take a page from their book because nobody hunts for a dead man. My retirement may seem coincidental, but I'd been talking about it for a while. Plus, we were *extremely* careful to make sure no one knew about our relationship," Madeline said.

"You put yourself at risk like that, for my dad?" Angel asked

"Yes," Madeline replied simply, looking at me with unconditional love in her eyes.

"Thank you," Destiny said.

"Yeah, thank you," Angel reiterated genuinely.

"I did it for selfish reasons, but you're welcome," Madeline replied smiling.

"So, where are you two headed, now that you don't have to look over your shoulder?" Lil' Boy asked.

"I'm not sailing off into the sunset while my son and grandson are out there somewhere," I replied.

"It's not a good idea for you to be directly involved in this, and I say that with all due respect," Bone stated, looking directly at me.

"Why is that?" I asked, fighting to keep my anger in check.

"Because Free is gonna kill, Royal," Angel said softly.

I didn't have to look at Free to know that her eyes were on me or to gauge how much truth there was to Angel's statement. She and I had already had this conversation back at the hotel.

"Free and I have already come to an agreement on that," I replied.

"And what would that be?" Bone asked, looking at Free.

"Unless Royal harms B.J., Free has agreed to let me deal with him. But, if he hurts your son she's gonna kill him," I replied, hating the taste those words left in my mouth.

"And you're gonna let her do that?" Angel asked, skeptically.

"I don't see how I have a choice," I said, honestly.

"He *knows* he doesn't have a choice," Free stated, still staring at me.

The Boss Man's Daughters 5

For a moment no one besides me and my oldest daughter spoke, and we did it without words. We understood each other on another level, and that had never concerned me until this very moment.

"We don't have time to waste, so let's get on the move," I suggested.

Aryanna

Chapter 16
~Royal~
One Week Later
Dubai

"B.J., eat your food," I demanded.

"No."

"B.J., I'm not playing with you, now eat your food," I said, pushing the plate with pizza on it towards him.

He didn't reach out for it like I'd hoped, but instead crossed his little arms over his chest defiantly and sat back in his chair. My frustration and impatience were approaching their limitations, which was gonna result in me whooping his ass again shortly. He'd gotten more spankings in the last week than he had in the last year and a half! I knew he was acting out and testing me because he missed Prince but he was gonna have to accept the fact that Prince was gone. It hurt me, too, but I knew there was no way I'd ever see him again, let alone get to raise him like he deserved. It was just me and B.J. now, and he would have to get used to it.

"B.J., you need to eat, buddy," I said, using a gentler tone.

"No, I want Prince and Tima," he declared stubbornly.

I had to count to ten to stop myself from screaming like a crazy person, not just because B.J. was being difficult, but because he'd said *her* name. Every time, I thought about Fatima, I wished I could kill her traitorous ass all over again! The betrayal was one thing, but the way she used me and manipulated me emotionally is what still had the wound open. I knew B.J. simply wanted what was familiar to him, especially given how isolated he was raised, but it still infuriated me to hear that bitch's name.

"You're gonna sit there until you eat," I said, getting up from the table and going into the living room.

Aryanna

It had been my intention to go back to my laptop to try and figure out what my next move should be, but instead, I ended up at the window enjoying the view. It wasn't as beautiful as the sunsets I'd witnessed in Africa but being forty floors up had me feeling like I could reach out and dip my finger in the burnt orange in the sky. We'd moved around so much since being forced to flee Africa, that I'd literally seen almost the whole world, but I felt like I hadn't seen any of it. I wasn't allowed to enjoy beauty for beauty's sake, and that was sad.

"Mr. Walker, I'm going to do my check now," Thomas announced from the front door of my hotel room.

"That's fine," I replied, without turning to look at him.

I could see the reflection of his stocky build, blond hair, and stern expression off the glass as he exited the room like clockwork, signaling it had been an hour since his last check.

After what had happened in Jamaica, I kept someone stationed in the room adjacent to mine, and I insisted on complete floor and perimeter checks every hour. I'd also hacked into the hotel's database, so I could see who all the current guests were, and who the new guests were that checked in. I kept a close eye on their camera footage too, because I wasn't about to be surprised by my sisters again.

Thinking about them drove me back to my laptop because I had to find a way to either eliminate them or neutralize their asses. The easiest way to keep them far away from B.J. and I was to simply go back to the United States, but I couldn't do that until the bullshit case against me was dropped. I'd hired the best legal team money could buy, but so far all I'd heard was *'be patient'*. I was *tired* of that shit. I still had no idea where my sisters were, I just knew they'd somehow managed to slip out of Jamaica and avoid capture. So, far they'd managed not to show up on anyone's radar in the countries I'd been monitoring that wouldn't extradite, but that would only last for so long.

Whenever they surfaced, I planned to send every hired hitta I could find at their mufuckin' necks. Not just because of the mercenaries that had been sent my way, but because of what they'd made me do to Fatima. Her blood was on their hands.

"Royal," B.J. called.

I could tell by his tone that he wasn't far away from tears and I *hated* that. Because whenever he cried I felt bad. Having to whoop him was the hardest thing, I'd ever done in my life, but discipline was necessary.

"Royal," he called again.

"What B.J.?"

"I done," he replied

I got up from the couch and went back into the dining room where I found half a slice of pizza left on his plate and the crust from the other slice. If it hadn't been for the sauce all over his face, I might've thought he'd made the food disappear another way. I'd wanted him to eat both slices, but I accepted this compromise and took the paper plate from in front of him. Being that I didn't feel safe going out in public all the time, I'd gotten a hotel room equipped to function like an apartment, complete with a working kitchen. I threw the plate in the trash and grabbed a Choco-taco ice cream sandwich from the freezer before going back into the dining room.

"Here," I said, opening the wrapper for him and sitting the sweet treat in front of him.

Almost any child his age would've been reaching for it before I could put it down, but B.J. just sat there looking at it.

"You don't want it?" I asked, thinking the threat of losing it would prompt him to take it.

He didn't move towards it though, he simply shook his head and climbed down from the table. The guilt I felt was consuming, and for the first time, it made me question whether I was making the right decisions. This had all started

137

with me wanting to do what was best for two little innocent boys, who I felt should never know the evils of the family they were born into. I'd just wanted them safe and happy, but my failure was evident in the hunch of B.J.'s shoulders as he walked away into the living room.

Somehow, I had to fix this situation. So, I picked up the ice cream, followed him into the living room and sat beside him on the couch.

"I miss Prince too, B.J., and I'm gonna do everything I can to bring him home," I promised.

"When," he asked, looking up at me.

"Soon buddy, real soon. I know you miss him and Fatima a lot just like I do, but you still have me, and I love you very much. Okay?" I asked, putting my arm around him and pulling him close.

"Kay."

"Good, now you take this ice cream, while I find us a movie to watch," I said, passing him his dessert while grabbing my laptop.

I pulled up the Minions movie and we spent the next couple hours in the land of animation. B.J. literally laughed himself to sleep, and once the movie went off, I sat there watching his little chest rise and fall. His sleep was so peaceful, and it was my responsibility to bring peace to every part of his life. Once I carried him to bed, I came back to the living room to figure out how to do just that. Even though it was like beating a dead horse, I went back to trying to find their location.

"Where would I be if I were them?" I wondered aloud.

Asking that question put an idea in my head that actually made me smile and realize, I'd been looking at this situation wrong all along. I had what Free so desperately wanted, and even though, I would never actually use B.J. as bait, I could trick Free into thinking she'd be at the right place at the right time. In reality, she'd be where I wanted her to be and there was no doubt in my mind, she'd have the rest of the crew with her.

The only question I had left was where did I want to set my trap. The options were limitless because I had no doubt Free would travel anywhere for her son, including the most dangerous place of all. With a plan of sheer genius formulating in my mind, I fired off an email to my legal team in Washington, D.C. and followed it up with one to the security firm I'd hired. My plan was simple, yet complicated.

It was complicated because I was preparing to lure Free to the one country that wanted both of our heads, and she had no choice except to show up or risk losing B.J. to the system. It was simple because I was truly about to put a mother's love to the test. My lawyer's response was almost immediate, which didn't surprise me, because they were just opening for business on that side of the world. The message sent in response to mine was short and direct, telling me I'd lost my mind. I quickly fired one back assuring them I hadn't. I was simply trying to check the government's temperature with regards to the saying *'Innocent till proven guilty'*.

The message I received from the security firm was more accommodating and had me transferring money into their business account immediately. Once that task was complete I sent another e-mail to my lawyers assuring them, I had no intention of seeing my proposed plan through to its conclusion, at least not until they'd brokered a deal. I did, however, want the government to *think* I was going through with my proposed plan. A few minutes later, I received their reply, and this time we were all on the same page. For the first time in a while, I felt like I was playing chess and not checkers.

I shut my laptop down and went to bed, embracing my first good night of sleep since I'd left, Africa. When I awoke in the morning I found beauty in everything around me, from the sun shining through the floor to ceiling window of my bedroom to the smell of breakfast cooking. After putting on some shorts I made my way into the kitchen, and there was beauty in abundance.

"And you are?" I asked the woman hard at work at the stove.

She was about five foot six, maybe one-hundred and fifteen pounds on her petite frame, wearing a white flowing summer dress with no shoes. Her complexion was something that Willy Wonka would've loved for his chocolate bars, and when she turned around to face me, I saw that her light brown eyes made her even more striking.

"I'm Seraphina, and you must be, Royal. Nice to meet you," she replied, stepping towards me and offering me her hand to shake.

I took it, immediately inhaling the scent of some exotic fragrance wafting in the air between us.

"Did your boss tell you what I need?" I asked.

"He said you'd provide the specifics, but generally speaking you wanted a security slash nanny person in the form of a female for your son."

Every word she spoke had me falling in love with her British accent, but I managed to stay focused on business.

"That's exactly what I need. You'll be staying here with B.J., while I'm away on business, and you're *not* to leave this hotel room. If anything happens to him, you will pay the ultimate price understand?"

"Understood," she replied, unflinchingly.

"Good. What are you cooking?"

"French toast, eggs, and bacon. I trust that you're hungry," she said, smiling as she turned back to the stove.

"With everything smelling this good it would be impossible for me not to be. I'm gonna see if B.J. is awake," I replied, turning around to find B.J. actually standing right behind me.

I couldn't tell if he was rubbing the sleep out of his eyes or trying to get a better look at Seraphina, but he was unusually quiet.

"Hey, buddy, you hungry?" I asked, picking him up.

He didn't say anything, but he did nod his head while keeping his eyes locked on Seraphina's movements. I took him into the dining room with me and sat him down in the chair next to mine. A few minutes later, Seraphina came in carrying two plates and put them in front of us.

"Do you want me to cut up your French toast B.J.?" She asked.

Again, he spoke no words but nodded his approval.

"You're not gonna cut mine up, too?" I asked.

I had no idea where that comment came from, but it made her laugh, and the sound was melodic.

"I think you can handle that yourself," she replied, before disappearing back towards the kitchen.

When she returned moments later she was carrying her own plate and a pitcher of orange juice.

"Do you want juice, B.J.?" she asked.

"Yeah," he replied softly.

"Oh, so, you *can* talk," she said, smiling at him in a way that made him show a lot of his teeth in return.

"So, Seraphina, tell me about yourself," I said, digging into my food.

I was pleasantly surprised to find that the food tasted as good as it smelled.

"Well, I'm twenty-three, born and raised in London. I'm a workaholic, and my aim is incredible no matter what weapon I'm using," she replied, before taking a bite of her own food.

"Does being a workaholic mean you're good at your job?"

"I'd like to think so, I mean I've never lost a client," she replied, casually.

"That's reassuring, but you need to know the type of people you're protecting my little man from."

I spent the next fifteen minutes giving her a rundown on my sisters and the men in their lives, making sure not to spare any details when illustrating their treachery. To underestimate them in any way would guarantee death. I'd hate to see Seraphina end up as another notch on a gun. When I was done speaking I gauged her expression, looking for signs of uncertainty or fear, but finding none.

"Seems like I've heard of their work before, even on my side of the pond. I can handle protecting B.J. though," she said, confidently.

"You sure?"

"I'm positive, they've never met a bitch like me."

Chapter 17
~Free~
Russia

The moment a hand clamped down on my mouth roughly fear instantly shot into my veins, making me reach for the pistol, I slept with under my pillow. Before I could find the comforting rubber grip of my Glock, I felt his tongue wave an intimate hello to my clit, and my fear was immediately replaced with trust. My body, once rigid in preparation to fight, now surrendered to the will of the man between my trembling thighs. My hands went to his head, encouraging his tongues exploration because it was giving me a warmth the coldest winters couldn't disturb.

When an involuntary moan arose from my throat, I felt his grip tighten around my lips to keep it silenced, and I knew it was because our daughter was awake, but he was determined to finish what he'd started. Using his mouth alone, he took me to heights above the clouds, sucking my clit like it was the sweetest piece of chocolate, before using his tongue to catch my pussy juices so they could melt in his mouth. After cumming twice in ten minutes, I thought keeping quiet would be possible, but once he pushed his dick deep inside of me, I *knew* it was a lost cause.

I could tell by the look on Bone's face, that he knew it too because he quickly put his hand in my mouth, allowing me to bite down with every punishing stroke he delivered. By the third blow, I couldn't keep my back on the mattress, and I could taste his blood flowing into my mouth, but that didn't make him take it any easier. In fact, it motivated him. The destruction his throbbing dick was trying to put on my pussy walls built my climax swiftly, leaving me no time to prepare before the best part of death overtook me again.

Aryanna

I wanted to beg him to pause for a second and let me catch my breath, but before I could stop shaking he'd flipped me onto my stomach and pinned me to the bed with pounding blows that I could feel in my stomach.

"Unh," I moaned lovingly before he shoved his hand back into my mouth and continued riding me savagely.

Every moment that passed Bone made it clearer, he was in charge, and he was determined to bust this pussy open like wildflower. I couldn't say it with words, but *God* I loved him! He alternated his speed between painfully slow and break-a-bitches-neck fast until we finally came together twenty minutes later. I was so beyond words all I could do was lay there on my face, amazed by how long it took my body to stop rocking even after he'd laid down beside me.

"Do I even wanna *know* what that was about?" I asked, weakly.

"Just because I love you, and it's Tuesday."

His response made me laugh, which was his intent, but also a clear deflection because I could tell he had something on his satellite.

"I'm not calling complete bullshit on your reasoning, but I feel like you literally just fucked me like you won't see me again," I said.

The laughter that had been dancing in his eyes moments ago quickly vanished, and was replaced by a steel curtain, that hid all his emotions away from prying eyes.

"Hey, don't do that, don't shut me out. I'm your wife and best friend, so you don't get to do that with me," I said, putting my hand on his cheek.

"I know who you are, Freedom. It's just—"

"Just what? You wanna ask me to sit on the sideline? Go ahead and ask."

"But you won't do that because it's not who you are," he replied.

"Exactly, but it's not who *you* are to not ask me, anyway. That doesn't mean we have to fight about it."

Despite my words, I could tell he wanted to fight about it, though. Kamile dying and me getting shot had been a reality check for him because it proved that while we may be lucky, we weren't invincible.

"Baby, you're not at one-hundred percent right now, so I think you should let us handle things from here," he reasoned.

"After that dick down I just took I think I can handle *anything*," I replied smiling.

He didn't so much as crack a smirk which meant, he was determined to have this very serious conversation, right now.

"My shoulder is only a little sore, it's no big deal," I said, confidently.

"It's only been a week, and gunshots don't heal in a week, not even for the immortal Walker sisters. You think you're fine, but so did, Kamile."

"That's not fair," I replied, quickly, turning over on my back, so I could look at the ceiling instead of the truth in his eyes,

"Fair—what's not fair is that Prince now has to grow up without the mother, who loved him more than anything in the world. Will it be fair to subject B.J. to the same fate?"

"If this wasn't *about,* B.J., I'd say you're absolutely right, but we're talking about, *our* son. *Our* son who didn't even recognize me when he saw me and is right now somewhere in the world with a boy that is *seriously* unhinged. I *have* to find him and bring him home don't you get that?" I asked, emotionally, fighting my tears.

At first when he put his arms around me I didn't relax my body, but eventually, the battle with my tears was lost, and I took comfort from the only person who truly understood my pain. I had no idea how we'd gone from earth tilting sex to me being an emotional basket case, but I loved having someone I could go through it at all with. He held me without saying another word, as we laid there listening to our daughter entertain herself until her sounds turned to those of impatient hunger.

"I'll get her bottle," I said, sliding from beneath the comforter and pulling Bone's t-shirt on.

I was surprised to find no one in the kitchen of Kamile's penthouse apartment, but I was grateful for the moments of solitude, while I warmed Grace's bottle. I could still remember the days when I'd done the same for B.J., and the fact that I'd lost those moments too soon strengthened my resolve not to rest until I had my son back.

"Morning sis," Angel said, coming into the kitchen, kissing me on the cheek before going to the refrigerator.

"Morning."

"What's wrong?" she asked, over her shoulder.

"What makes you think something's wrong?"

"Because these walls ain't exactly the thickest, plus you still like *good* sex, but you allowed me to kiss you without cracking a remark about where my mouth has been. That leads me to believe, you're not in the bubbly playful mood that accompanies *good sex*, so something's wrong. Spill it," she insisted, leaning against the counter, sipping a strawberry orange sunny delight.

Despite her analysis being quick and accurate, I didn't know whether to reply like she *didn't* just admit to hearing Bone and I fucking or walk out of the room embarrassed.

"I was just thinking about B.J.," I replied, truthfully.

"Oh, that explains it. We're gonna get him back, Free, you can't believe anything else."

"Yeah, I know," I replied, softly, taking the bottle from the microwave and heading back to my room.

When I came through the door I passed the bottle to Bone because he was already holding Grace, and went to take a shower. I stayed under the hot water and let it beat my scalp until my fingers looked like they belonged to a ninety-year-old lady. When I stepped out I felt refreshed, like I'd sufficiently tucked my emotions away enough not to trip over them. I'd expected to find Bone still in the bedroom, but the room was empty except for Grace who was fast asleep in her crib. I spent a few moments watching her before I put some clothes on and followed the smell of food back to the kitchen, where I discovered the whole house was awake. Walking in it felt like one of those teeny bopper high movies where everyone stops talking and stares, but I wasn't as uncomfortable as I was curious.

"Please, don't stop talking on my account," I said, sarcastically.

"On the contrary, we were waiting for you to finish your shower. You need to see this," my sister said, pushing a laptop towards the open seat at the table.

I looked around at everyone as I moved forward, trying to gauge the mood, whatever I was about to see had caused, but everyone was wearing expressions you'd expect to find on the casino floor. When I sat down and pulled the laptop closer I saw a video of a news conference waiting to be played. Seeing Royal's name in bold print next to the law firm of Stricker and Figalmen put a knot in my stomach because I was positive this wasn't gonna be good. Still, I hit the button to watch, and five minutes later, I was completely dumbfounded.

"Let me see if I'm understanding this correctly. Royal, is planning to turn himself into the United States government to prove his innocence on the terrorist allegations, and he's saying that he can prove Bone blew up the F.B.I. building?" I said, looking around the table at everyone.

"More or less," Bone replied, gravely.

"How the fuck does that make any kind of sense?" I asked, lost as to what Royal's motivation was.

"It doesn't make sense because even with his lawyers trying to use his age and lack of any previous criminal involvement as his best defense, the evidence is still solid. I've seen it," Madeline replied, from her position at the stove.

"I know it's solid, we *created* it! Royal's not dumb, so there has to be a plan," I said, still shaking my head in confusion.

"So, far we've only been able to come up with one thing that plays," Destiny said, reluctantly.

When I looked around the table again, I had a bad feeling I wasn't gonna like the theory I was about to hear.

"Fill me in," I replied.

"If Royal turns himself in that means B.J. goes into foster care, and since we're all wanted no one would be able to get him out," Bone stated.

For a moment, I just looked at him because that was the dumbest shit I'd heard in my life. The problem was that as the seconds ticked past loudly in my mind, the conclusion my husband had drawn didn't seem so dumb or crazy, only cruel.

"He-he wouldn't subject B.J. to the system, he's smart enough to know that's not good," I said.

"Maybe to his way of thinking B.J. being raised by foster parents is still better than being with you, or him now that he's a fugitive as well," Angel replied.

"No—no," I said, shaking my head.

The thought of my son being raised by strangers who didn't know him and *couldn't* love him the way I could made me sick to my stomach.

"Listen, Free—"

"Dad *don't*! If he turns my son over to the Goddamn system *I'm burying* him, and anyone who tries to stop me," I growled, angrily.

It hadn't been my intention to hurt my dad, but I could tell by the expression riding his face, that I'd done exactly that.

"It doesn't have to come to that," Madeline stated calmly, bringing two pans of eggs and sausage to the table.

The Boss Man's Daughters 5

"If you've got something to say spit it the fuck out or shut your mouth," I replied, with barely controlled rage at the nerve of this bitch.

I could tell by the way her eyes snapped to mine, she wasn't accustomed to being talked to the way I'd talked to her. I was sure my facial expression stated loud and clear, I didn't give a fuck.

"Like I told you when we first met, despite helping your dad breakout. I'm not a fugitive or even suspected of any wrongdoing. In fact, I'm an upstanding citizen with an impeccable service record and *many* connections inside the crooked government. I can call in some favors," Madeline said, before going back to the stove and turning off the burners.

I didn't address what she said until she took a seat beside my dad.

"So, what are you saying? You'll be able to keep an eye on my son? By then it'll be too *late*, he'll be in the system," I said, feeling frustrated and helpless.

"What I'm saying is that *I'll* go get your son," Madeline clarified.

"Sweetheart, a move like that *could* draw suspicion. I mean, I don't think anyone will believe it's a coincidence that you're wanting to take guardianship of my grandson. They'd think you knew where my daughters were," my dad replied.

"It doesn't matter what they *think* they know Jonathan, it's only what they can prove. Furthermore, favors aren't asked for or given in public, that type of stuff is handled behind closed doors. I'll be able to get B.J. back quietly, trust me," Madeline said, taking my father's hand in hers.

I'd never seen him allow anyone other than Kamile to use his first name, and the way he was looking at Madeline definitely said he felt some type of way towards her. I couldn't tell if that was clouding his judgment, but I was looking at this clearly.

"You think you're just gonna walk away with my son without anyone noticing? Royal, has gone public and that's something the U.S. government hasn't even done yet," I said.

"True, but *he'll* be in the limelight, not your son. I can get him back, Free. You've gotta trust me, though," Madeline replied.

I wanted so bad to believe her, but she saw my son as some innocent little boy, that would receive mercy and understanding from a country incapable of either. B.J. wouldn't be seen as a poor little black boy in need of a good home. He'd be seen as a child with the last name Walker, making him a killer before he even understood the meaning of the word. The sins of not just the parents, but of B.J.'s entire family, would fall on the head of my beautiful little boy, and I couldn't let that happen.

"I trust you, Madeline. I just don't think you understand how my son will be viewed just because of who his family is," I said, honestly.

"Free's right," Angel acknowledged.

"My job for the marines was intelligence gathering so do you really believe, I don't know the consequences that come with your last name? Just because your dad doesn't talk about it. Do you think he wasn't tortured for being who he was, or that I didn't have to *see* the results of that torture? Free, when you were in the hospital, I told you, you'd *never* get a fair trial, only a fair execution. I know that to be true simply because of how hated your entire family is. It's for that reason, we can't gamble on what happens with your son. I have to go get him, let me do this," Madeline insisted passionately.

"She's right, babe," Bone replied, looking at me.

"And it's not like we'll be doing nothing on this end sweetheart. We've still got the move to make in London. According to Royal's lawyers, we've got forty-eight hours. So,

Madeline can catch a flight back to the states and we can focus on finding Royal ahead of time," my dad said.

"I'll stay with the kids," Destiny offered.

It was evident that this big ass dysfunctional family I was a part of was pulling together, stronger than ever, and I loved them for it. Madeline was new to all this, but she was proving she was down through the good, the bad, and the ugly. She had heart, and she was loyal. I was gonna put my faith in that.

"Okay, Madeline, but I hope you know what you're doing. For all our sakes."

Aryanna

Chapter 18
~Father-God~

"What are you looking at?" I asked Madeline.

I could tell she hadn't heard me come into the bedroom, we'd been sharing because she jumped at the sound of my voice, and the guilty expression on her face told me what she'd been doing. I closed the door quietly before crossing the room to sit beside her on the bed.

"I just talked to my mom," Madeline replied, passing me her phone.

Frozen on the screen was the smiling face of the most beautiful, little, light-skinned girl with mesmerizing green eyes, and a head full of reddish brown curls.

"How is she?" I asked.

"Mom says she's fine, but she misses me."

I could hear the sadness in Madeline's tone, and it broke my heart.

"I think you should go see her," I encouraged.

"We agreed to wait until this situation was cleared up, or at least more stable. I don't think it's either of those things right now."

"You're right, but time is something you can never get back, so you shouldn't take it for granted. You're already going back to the U.S. anyway, so why not make a stop in, Kansas City?" I asked.

I could tell by the longing in her eyes that she wanted to do just that, but something was holding her back.

"I want to see her—I *need* to see her, but I feel guilty because, Free, doesn't have her son. Being away from our daughter for this long is the hardest thing I've ever had to endure, but I can't express that or justify a visit when, Free, is waking up in hell *every single day*. Not to mention, the fact that no one knows you and I even *have* a daughter," she replied, with growing frustration.

I'd always known how compassionate and honest Madeline was, and right now, both of those qualities was causing turmoil inside of her. Initially, keeping the secret about our four-month-old daughter had been an absolute necessity for obvious reasons, but we'd agreed once we'd started our new life together it would be without deception. One thing after another had happened which always made the timing for announcing our baby seem inappropriate, and it was clearly taking its toll on Madeline.

"Sweetheart, you don't need to feel guilty, and Free wouldn't want you to either. As for justification, you're a mother, who misses her child. That's the only reason you need to go see our daughter. Understand?" I asked, looking her in the eyes.

"But it's not fair because Free—"

"Hold that thought," I said, getting up and going to the door.

I quietly pulled it opened and hollered down the hall for Free to come to my room. Once she got there I closed the door behind her and gave her Madeline's phone.

"She's beautiful, but—I don't understand why you called me in here to see this picture," Free said slowly.

"Jonathan don't," Madeline whispered.

"Her name is, Truth Love Parker, and she's four months old," I said, watching Free closely, ignoring Madeline.

"Parker, so is this your daughter?" Free asked Madeline, smiling.

"Y-yeah," Madeline replied, cautiously.

"How come you didn't say anything before, she's so—" Free's voice trailed off as she examined the picture closer, tapping the screen to make it bigger.

Suddenly her eyes went back to Madeline and then swung back in my direction.

"You always make beautiful babies," Free said, neutrally.

"Strong-willed too," I replied.

"Why didn't you tell us?" Free asked.

"That was on me. I just didn't feel right given everything you're going through with your own son," Madeline replied, honestly.

Free continued to stare at me a moment longer before moving to sit beside Madeline on the bed.

"To be part of this life, part of this family. You have to understand, the good things and joyous occasions are the only thing that gets us through the darkness hovering around us like a black cloud. Every day without my son is one filled with unexplainable pain, but that wouldn't stop me from celebrating another addition to our family. You know first-hand that a lot of people would love nothing more than to make all of us extinct. So, growing our bloodline is a wonderful thing. And it makes us family forever," Free said, putting her arm around Madeline and pulling her into a hug.

I wanted to go to them and join in, but this was their moment, so I stood silently and observed.

"Thank you for being so understanding," Madeline replied emotionally.

"You don't need to thank me. You've just given me more of a reason to fuck with you. I can't wait to meet little, Truth," Free said.

"My plan is to bring her back when I bring B.J. home," Madeline replied.

"It is?" I asked, surprised by her revelation.

"Yes, it is, she needs to finally meet her dad, and the huge family she was born into," Madeline insisted.

"I agree," Free chimed in.

"Good, now that that's settled I need to get ready to catch my flight," Madeline said standing.

"And I need to finish making our travel plans to London," Free stated, giving Madeline her phone back, then standing up, coming towards me.

When I opened my arms, she stepped into my embrace with the same enthusiasm she'd had since she was old enough to walk. I could see the unshed tears of happiness in Madeline's eyes as I held Free. I felt hope for what was to come once the dust settled.

"Congratulations old man, you've done it again," Free said, laughing.

"Watch it calling me old," I replied, squeezing her tightly.

Even after I'd let her go she kept laughing as she left the room.

"I can't believe you did that," Madeline said, once we were alone again.

"Believe it. One thing you'll learn about this crazy ass family is that we give love and loyalty in abundance," I replied, moving towards her until we were standing face to face.

"I love that you've made me feel like part of the family from the beginning," she said, putting her arms around my neck, pulling my lips down to meet hers.

The kiss was sweet and soft, but passionate enough to have me unbuttoning her jeans, so I could slide my hands into her panties in search of the keys to reaching the next level.

"B-babe, I've gotta book my f-flight," she mumbled, pulling on my hand weakly.

"We've got time, trust me," I replied, smiling devilishly as I pushed my middle finger slowly inside of her.

I found her to be soaking wet and hot, making it clear without words that she was ready, willing, and able. I pushed her jeans and panties down over her hips and nudged her backward onto the bed. She put her legs straight in the air expecting me to pull her jeans off, but instead, I kneeled on the bed, pulled my dick out of my shorts, and drove it into her swiftly.

"Oh, Jesus," she moaned.

"You can call me, God," I whispered, wrapping my arms around her legs, keeping them close together, while feeding her slow, deep strokes. The sight of her beautiful eyes fighting to stay focused on me, had me pumping harder and swiveling my hips to ensure I hit her pussy walls front, back, and side to side. Every dive her body took was taunting me, daring me to take what I wanted, and that's exactly what I intended to do.

"J-J-J-Jon-a-than," she stuttered, as her body began shaking uncontrollably.

My insistent, unrelenting, pounding blows turned her shaking into an earthquake, that gave birth to a fast-moving volcano, and still, I gave her more. By leaning on her legs, I changed the angle while increasing my downward force, and that had the sounds of her splashing weirdness echoing throughout the room like a beautiful summer rain. My climax was just around the next corner, but I needed her with me in order to recreate the magic that made me a fiend for her love.

"Come for me," I demanded.

"N-n-no!"

She knew how much it turned me on when she resisted the inevitable. Without missing a stroke, I finally pulled her pants and panties off, tossing them to the floor. This allowed me to spread her legs while bending her in half, and give her the feeling that my dick was inches away from knocking her lungs through her mouth.

"Oh-oh, God!" She yelled, turning two different shades of red in the face.

She didn't have to tell me she was moments away from an orgasm because her body was singing like it was possessed by an R&B legend. A few short minutes later, I came hard enough to make my eyes water, and she followed me over the edge of complete fulfillment without hesitation. It took great effort for me to climb off her, but I knew if I didn't neither of us would accomplish anything more than multiple orgasms today.

"Pl-please don't be gone long," I panted, smiling at her.

"If I didn't need to, I wouldn't be leaving at all."

"Yo, pops, you done yet?" Destiny called from right outside our bedroom door.

The only way to describe the expression on Madeline's face was mortified. If I'd thought she'd been red in the face moments ago, that was *nothing* compared to now. I couldn't help laughing.

"That's *not* funny," she whispered fiercely, hitting me in the chest.

"It kinda is," I replied, getting out of bed.

"Don't you open that door, Jonathan Walker," she ordered, scrambling from the bed, making a mad dash to the bathroom.

I waited until I heard the shower turn on before I went to the door and partially opened it.

"For real, you just gonna stand at the door and listen?" I asked, Destiny and Angel.

"At least we waited until you two were done, considering you already went half on a baby," Angel replied, looking at me with daggers in her eyes.

"Run them pictures old man," Destiny demanded.

"I'll be out in a minute," I replied, closing the door on them.

I should've known Free wouldn't keep a secret that big from her sister, which meant I'd have to face the music. After grabbing Madeline's phone, I ventured out into the lion's den, finding Angel and Destiny sitting at the kitchen table. I sat down across from them, pulled up Madeline's photo gallery, and slid the phone to them.

"Oh *wow*, she's absolutely adorable," Angel gushed, smiling.

"She looks like the baby pictures I've seen of you Angel, only lighter," Destiny commented.

"What's her name?" Angel asked.

"Oh, Free didn't tell you that," I replied, sarcastically.

My comments earned me hard looks from both of them causing me to raise my hands in quick surrender.

"Her name is, Truth Love Parker," I said.

"That nose and those cheeks make her a Walker all day long," Destiny said, swiping through the pictures.

"Well her first and middle names definitely fit the mold of the rest of the family, and I'm assuming that was your idea," Angel said, looking at me.

"Actually, it was Madeline's decision. She picked it because she said our daughter was made because of true love, and no matter what happened, she vowed to make sure she always knew that," I replied, smiling at the memory of that conversation.

"We don't keep secrets," Angel said, suddenly serious.

"Yeah, I know," I replied, not shying away from the penetrating stares they were leveling at me.

"Does Madeline know that?" Destiny asked.

"She wasn't doing it with malicious intent," I said.

"You taught us a long time ago that intent doesn't matter," Angel replied.

"You're right, I did. Madeline knows we don't keep secrets from each other in this family," I said.

They continued staring at me for a little while before going back to the pictures on Madeline's phone.

"Truth has a lot of love waiting for her when this is all over," Angel said, wishfully.

"That she does, which means we need to get this shit over sooner than later," I replied.

"We've got the address to the estate of, William Emerson, CEO of Emerson security firm in, London. I've already contacted our payroll, so they can hack into NASA without their knowledge," Destiny said.

Aryanna

"There's no question, he'll have the info we need, right?" I asked.

"No question," Angel reiterated.

"You all still talking about our beautiful baby sister, or have you got to the point of threatening to kick dad's ass if he keeps some shit from us again?" Free asked, joining us at the table.

"We've moved passed personal and we're on to business now, smartass," I replied, shaking my head.

"Cool, then, I'm just in time. Since Destiny volunteered to stay with the kids I think Big Baby should stay too for security purposes. That don't mean you spend all day on his dick or his face either, bitch," Free warned.

"Wait, your fucking, Big Baby? I thought you only liked women," I said.

"You're *sooo* late, dad," Angel replied.

"Can we stop discussing what I do with *my* vagina," Destiny said, clearly embarrassed.

"Okay, so that leaves me, Bone, Angel, Lil' Boy, and you dad going to London. It's not smart for everyone to arrive at once. So, I say we take the yacht tonight and once we make landfall we make three trips into the city," Free suggested.

"What about weapons?" I asked.

"We've got some, but there should be more at the strip club," Angel replied.

"Well since you're a familiar face why don't you go get them," Free said.

"A'ight, I'll take Lil' Boy and do that now," Angel said, getting up and leaving the kitchen.

On her way out, Madeline was coming in, and she sat next to me.

"You okay?" Destiny asked, smiling hard.

"Pause, you didn't wanna talk about what you do with *your* vagina, so don't get cute," I warned.

160

"Fair enough. You did make a beautiful baby, though, and I can't wait to meet her," Destiny said.

"Thank you," Madeline replied, shyly.

"Did you book your flight?" I asked Madeline.

"Yeah, I got one that leaves in an hour, because I'm headed to Kansas City first," she replied, looking at me to gauge my response.

I leaned over and kissed her softly on the forehead.

"Give our daughter that from me," I said.

"From us, too," Free said, hopping up, followed by Destiny.

They ran around the table and sandwiched Madeline between them, kissing her on both cheeks, and making her laugh until tears rolled from her eyes. They had me laughing too, and it felt good to do so because there probably wouldn't be anything to laugh about for a while.

"You got your bag packed?" I asked once we were all back under control.

"Yeah, are you going with me to the airport?" Madeline asked, taking my hand.

"Of course, I am. Girls, when I get back we're on the move. It's time to go make this family whole. As whole as possible anyway."

Aryanna

Chapter 19
~Angel~
London
Twenty-seven Hours Later

"Williammm," I sang softly, into the ear of the man I was standing over.

His eyes were slow to open, but when they did, they grew to the size of tea saucers immediately.

"Well, good morning sunshine, sorry to disturb your slumber, but we need to chat," I said, turning on his bedside lamp so he could get a better view of the shadows that had been occupying his room.

Lil' Boy was standing at the foot of the bed with one arm draped loosely around William's wife's shoulders, his chrome .45 gripped firmly in his hand for all to see. Free was standing at the other side of the bed next to Bone, cradling her Mossberg shotgun the same way she would her daughter. My dad was sitting behind me in a rocking chair, holding the Emerson's infant son, and once I was sure I had William's attention, I took a step back, so he could see everything.

"Who-who the fuck are you, and how did you get in my house?" William asked.

His tone was one of a man used to giving orders, but he was in for a rude awakening fucking with us.

"It was actually pathetically easy getting into your house considering that security is your life's work," Free said, shaking her head disapprovingly.

"Listen, I don't know *who* you are, or what the *fuck* you want, but—"

"Well, we can answer those questions easy enough, William. My name is Angel, this is my family," I said, gesturing around the room with my Ruger P92 pistol.

"And we're here for information," Free added, racking the slide on her shotgun.

"Information? What fucking information?" William asked, raising his voice.

I looked over at Lil' Boy, and he took his arm from around Rose Emerson's shoulders. Then he hit her with a vicious backhand slap that had her attacking the floor in a hurry.

"Watch your tone, William, or next time I won't be so nice," Lil' Boy threatened.

Rose's sudden cries had startled the baby, but my dad got him quieted down just as quickly.

"Okay, just tell me what you want and don't hurt my family," William replied, contritely.

"That's better. The information we want is pertaining to one of your clients. His name is, Royal Walker," I said.

"I-I don't have a client by that name," William stated, shaking his head unconvincingly.

Again, I looked towards Lil' Boy, and he reached down and lifted Rose off the floor by her hair.

"I don't have a client by the name, I swear!" William insisted vehemently.

"He's probably using a different name," Bone said.

"We're looking for someone who hired your firm for round the clock protection for himself and two small boys. This same client cost you two employees in Jamaica. I know that because I was the one who shot them down like dogs. Do you know who we're talking about now?" Free asked calmly.

I could tell by the look in William's brown eyes that he knew *exactly* who we were referring to, and he was starting to fully understand how bad shit was.

"What name did he give you?" Bone asked.

"Nyam Botani, he's supposed to be some type of African royalty," William replied.

"Far from it, he kidnapped my son," Free said.

"And mine," My dad chimed in.

"I-I didn't have anything to do with that. I run an honest business," William insisted.

"That's stretching the truth William, you rent hired guns to the highest bidder, so please don't act like you deserve the noble-piece prize," I said.

"Where's Nyam Botani?" Free asked.

"I-I don't know," William replied.

"Sure, you do, you know where everyone of your employees is at all times anywhere in the world," I said, confidently.

"Those records are kept in my office, not in my bedroom. Once we're open I can access them," he replied.

"Do you think we're stupid, Mr. Emerson?" my dad asked, patiently.

"No, but—"

"Good, because it would be a bad move to play us like we're stupid. And since I *know* you don't want to make any bad moves. I'm sure you won't have a problem accessing your companies records from your phone. Pass it to him, Angel, and watch his hand and his hesitation to take it. He looked at me, and looked around the room, his eyes lingering on first his child, then his wife.

"What happens when I give you what you want?" William asked softly.

"Then it's over," I replied, simply.

"Over how?" he questioned further.

"Just-just give them what they want!" Rose yelled, crying.

"You're upsetting the baby," My dad said, rocking the now crying infant.

"How do I know you won't just kill all of us once you get what you want?" William asked.

"Lil' Boy bring his wife over here, make her kneel in front of me, and give me your gun, too," My dad demanded.

Aryanna

I didn't know what he planned to do, but I knew it had the potential to be life-changing. I watched as my dad sat the baby up on his knee after accepting the gun from Lil' Boy, with bored on his face as the crying blond woman was put on her knees in front of him.

"William, I want you to listen to me very carefully. If you don't do *exactly* as my daughter tells you, I'm gonna kill your wife. Now I know that might not mean shit to you because you have a sexy little mistress. But, when I kill your wife, your son will die too, because I'll use his head for a silencer," my dad said calmly and carefully wedging the barrel of the pistol in the baby's mouth.

Then he flipped the safety off. It was a good thing I wasn't looking at William because I knew my eyes were wide with surprise. I hadn't seen this coming, but I knew beyond the shadow of a doubt that Father-God meant what he said, and he wouldn't be preparing himself.

"William, *please*!" Rose begged, almost hysterical.

"Okay, okay, I'll do it," William agreed, making his fingers fly over the screen of his phone.

Ninety seconds later, William was turning the phone for me to see.

"Okay, so it looks like Mr. Botani is scheduled to arrive in London this afternoon before hopping a flight to the United States. He's got a five-man team," I said, looking back at my dad.

"William, what can I do to ensure that you don't tip Mr. Botani, or your employees, off about our presence here in London?" my dad asked.

"I-I won't say anything, I swear," he replied, readily.

The look my dad gave me told me just how much he believed what he was being told. I turned back to William, raised my pistol, and fired a single shot that left his brains on the headboard. His wife's screams were entwined with the muffled cries of her son, but the expression on my dad's face remained calm and nonchalant.

"Congratulations Mrs. Emerson, you've just inherited your husband's security firm, and quite a nice estate to go with it. I want to talk to you for a minute, parent to parent, can we do that?" My dad asked.

Rose Emerson was beyond words for the moment, so all she could do was nod her head in agreement.

"Good. I want you to know, we didn't come here with the intent to harm your child, or you really, but as a parent, I'm sure you can understand if the choice is between my child and yours, it's not really a choice. We have the information we came for, which means we can now save those important to us. If you want to save your son, all you have to do is agree to never repeat what has happened here today. Can you do that?" My dad asked.

"Y-yes, I swear, I swear," Rose replied, crying uncontrollably.

For two long minutes, my dad sat there, staring dispassionately at the newly grieving widow with the pistol still very much in her crying son's jaws. When I looked around the room I could tell that none of us had a clue how this was gonna end.

"I believe you," my dad said finally, removing the gun and handing her baby over to her. I could see the relief in the slump of her shoulders, but they went tense again just as quickly when my dad put the gun to her forehead.

"Rose don't make me come back here," he said softly.

After a few moments, he pulled the gun away and stood up, signaling that it was time to go. I put Williams phone in my pocket and walked over to Rose.

"Give me your hand," I demanded.

She raised her right-hand palm up like we were in a Planet of the Apes movie, and she was signaling her submission. It would've been comical if this situation wasn't so serious. I placed my pistol in her hand and wrapped her fingers around it to ensure the transference of her fingerprints. Since

I was wearing gloves the only prints that existed on this gun were hers.

"Just in case you forget that the people in this room ain't to be fucked with. This gun is added insurance should you choose to open your dick suckers. The spouse is always the prime suspect, remember that," I said, leaving her kneeling on the floor, sobbing with her son.

After our task was completed we exited the house and disappeared with the rising of the sun. It was an hour's drive back to our safe house in the countryside outside of the city, and despite us all being tired there was still more work to do.

"Is there any food in this spot?" I asked, flopping down on the couch beside Lil' Boy.

"I think Free went to check," Bone replied, joining us in the living room and sitting on the couch across from us.

The safe house was actually a cabin with an open floor plan, that made the small space seem bigger. It shouldn't have surprised me that my dad had connections on this continent too, but it did.

"Anybody else want a drink?" My dad asked, coming into the room with a bottle of Brandy in his fist.

When no one offered to join him, he sat in the cushy leather chair that was pushed up against a wall and tipped the bottle to his mouth. I could tell he had a lot on his mind, and I wouldn't begin to know which problem his thoughts were circling around first, but I had a burning question.

"Would you have done it, dad?" I asked, with morbid curiosity.

He took another healthy swig of liquor, before turning his tired eyes on me.

"Is that a real question?" he retorted.

"Yeah, I mean that little boy couldn't have been much older than, Truth," I replied.

"Or much older than B.J. before Royal took him. If you're asking me if I relished the idea of killing an innocent child. You should already know the answer to that question.

But, if you're asking if I would've pulled the trigger, the answer is without hesitation," he said, before taking another drink.

An awkward silence filled the room following his statement, but I understood that my dad was only focused on bringing a peaceful resolution to this crisis within *his* family. Nobody else's life, not even a child's, could or would matter when it came to us, especially considering that if this went bad he'd lose a son.

"There's no food worth eating, so somebody is gonna have to go out and get something," Free said, sitting down beside Bone.

"We can worry about that in a minute, we need to strategize the next phase of our plan," my dad replied.

"According to the info on the late, Mr. Emerson's phone Royal will be arriving at a flat owned by the security firm at about five p.m. I think we should already be inside waiting on him," I said.

"Give me the address so I can check out the layout," Free said, pulling out her phone.

I dug William's phone out of my pocket and recited the address while pulling up a geo map of the location myself.

"Angel, I think you and dad should post up at the café across the street. Me, Bone, and Lil' Boy will be waiting for Royal and his entourage inside the flat," Free said.

"Why are me and dad on the street?" I asked.

"Because with the right clothing you'll blend in better, and Royal wouldn't recognize dad if he was standing right in front of him," Free replied logically.

"Oh. I guess you're right. So, how is this going down once they arrive?" I asked.

I watched my dad give Free a look before taking another sip from the liquor bottle, but he didn't say anything.

"We use the element of surprise and do our best to end this shit peacefully," Free replied, still looking at my dad.

Aryanna

"We all need a few hours of sleep before we make our next move," Lil' Boy said, standing up and holding out his hand to me.

I took it, allowing him to pull me to my feet and lead me to one of the bedrooms in the back of the cabin. He didn't say anything once the door was closed behind us, but I could tell he had something on his mind.

"What is it?" I asked, sitting on the queen-sized bed, motioning for him to join me.

"I've got a bad feeling about this," he admitted, taking my hand.

"Would you like to be more specific, babe? What's giving you bad vibes?"

"Other than the fact that, Royal, is completely unpredictable. Your dad and Free are clearly wanting to handle this situation differently. Free may have said the right thing out there a moment ago, but in real life, she wants to put a bullet in, Royal, and be done with it," he replied.

"You should be absolutely sure of that, but I'm not. He's still our brother, and my sister hasn't forgotten that," I said.

"Baby you know your sisters better than anyone, and you know that Free has no use and no patience for anyone she can't trust. She'll never trust Royal again, so with that being the case why would she let him live?"

His question was not only logical but valid, too. I didn't have an answer for him. People made mistakes, and when you loved them you could find a way to forgive them. I didn't know that the same could be said when it came to rebuilding trust. Trust was the difference between life and death out here in these streets. If I was being honest I knew Free would always feel like she had too much to lose to trust, Royal. Brother or no brother, that relationship wasn't worth it to her.

"If you're right, then you're gonna have to be on point when this shit goes down," I said.

"What can I do?"

The Boss Man's Daughters 5
"Whatever it takes to keep, Free, from shooting him."

Aryanna

Chapter 20
~Royal~
London

"Thomas have you heard back from your boss yet?" I asked, looking out through the rearview passenger's window at the busy streets of London.

"No sir, I haven't, but I plan to check in with him as soon as we get to the flat," he replied.

"I'd like to get something to eat before we tuck in for the night," I said, pulling my phone from my pocket.

"Where would you like to eat?" Thomas asked.

"McDonald's will be fine," I replied, texting Seraphina for the millionth time to check on B.J. It felt weird to be away from him, especially since I hadn't let him out of my sight since losing Prince.

I knew that making this next move was crucial to ensuring that B.J. had the best future, though. So, I would deal with being away from him for a couple of days.

"Why are we stopping?" I asked, noticing that Thomas was pulling the Range Rover to the curb.

"Just waiting for the rest of the team to make it through the light, sir. I've already alerted them of our detour, they'll be right behind us the entire way. Would you like to go into the restaurant or go through the drive-thru?"

"The drive-thru will be fine, and I want a quarter pounder value meal," I replied.

"We call that the Royal with chest," Thomas said, smiling.

I returned his smile like he was telling me something I didn't know. I was secretly hoping he didn't want to engage in small talk. I hadn't employed a five-man team, because I was lonely or pressed for conversation, so as far as I was concerned, Thomas could talk to his partner riding shotgun or one of the three in the truck behind us. To increase the chances of him not talking to me I chose to call Seraphina instead of continuing to text.

"Yes, Mr. Walker?" she answered, on the first ring.

"You can call me, Royal. How is everything?"

"Well, right now, we're curled up on the couch watching a movie and eating popcorn," she replied.

"Don't let him eat too much junk or he won't eat dinner," I instructed.

"Royal."

"I know, I know, I'm micromanaging, but I can't help it," I admitted.

Her laughter was instant and effortless, making me smile in a way that wouldn't have been possible if she'd just come out and called me ridiculous.

"Has he been good?" I asked.

"Better than any two-year-old I've ever met. He even says please and thank you, which means you raised him to have good manners, and that's something most parents over-look these days."

"Yeah, well, I was raised by a single mother who be-lieved men lacked manners. She was determined her only son wouldn't end up like those *'nothing ass niggas'*. I guess enough of that philosophy rubbed off on me to be passed down to my, little man," I replied.

"Thank god for *that*. B.J. is good though, and he's in great hands, so you don't have to worry so much. As hard as it obviously is for you to be away from him. I know you wouldn't do it unless you had some very important business to handle. So, if you focus on that you can get back to him sooner," she said, gently.

I knew she was right, but it still didn't take away from the anxiety I felt from not having him by my side. I realized that even though, I hadn't been raising B.J. to view me as his father I definitely felt responsible for him, like he was my son. I may not have had a father to lead by example in regards of how to love, but I felt like my unconditional love for B.J. was how a dad should feel.

"You're right, and I'll *try* to take your advice. Just tell him, I love him," I replied.

"You can tell him, hold on while I put you on speaker phone. Okay, go ahead," she said.

"Hey, buddy, I love you."

"Love you, too!" B.J. yelled excitedly.

"Be good for Seraphina, I'll be back soon, okay?"

"Kay!" he yelled.

"Thanks, Seraphina, I needed that," I confessed.

"You're welcome, now go to work," she replied, disconnecting.

Hearing my little guy's voice did make me feel better. Now I could definitely focus on what needed to be done. I went to work on my phone checking to see if there had been any sightings of my sisters or their niggas, but I didn't get far before we pulled up to the drive-thru. Nourishment became my top priority, but I couldn't even enjoy that because as soon as I bit into my sandwich both Thomas and Paul's phones started going off relentlessly.

"Is there a problem?" I asked, looking out of the back window to make sure the others Range Rover was still behind us.

"It seems that Mr. Emerson has been murdered," Thomas replied, in disbelief.

"Murdered? When and by who?" I asked, shocked.

"Sometime this morning, and it's not clear, yet who did it, but his wife Rose is being questioned as we speak," Thomas replied.

"Rose wouldn't kill, William," Paul stated, in a matter of fact tone.

"I agree, but it happened in their house, so the police are automatically gonna look at her," Thomas said.

"Was it a home invasion type of situation? Was Mr. Emerson the only victim?" I asked, curiously.

Aryanna

"There were no signs of forced entry, and yes he was the only person killed despite his wife and infant son being home sleeping," Thomas replied.

Hearing this made me breathe a little easier because my thoughts had immediately gone to my estranged family somehow being behind, William Emerson's death. They were definitely resourceful enough to make that kind of move, but if it were them no one would've left that house breathing.

"The vice president of the company wants all employees to check-in via FaceTime. So, we're heading to the flat where we can take care of that," Thomas informed me.

"That's fine, but this won't affect our travel plans, right?" I asked, focusing on the play I'd set in motion.

"It shouldn't. We've been hired to perform a service and Mr. Emerson prided himself on always getting the job done," Thomas said.

Hearing this was music to my ears because failure at this particular task wasn't acceptable. It took us twenty minutes to pull up in front of the flat, that would be my home for the night. I'd managed to finish my food while reading the story online about the late, William Emerson. One shot to the head was quick and easy, so maybe it was his wife. Had it been, an enemy torture probably would've definitely been on the menu.

"The rest of the team is gonna inspect the flat and secure it before we go in," Paul said.

I wanted to ask if all that was necessary, but I'd learned to let them handle their work without interference. After five minutes though, I was feeling impatient.

"What's the holdup, I thought—"

My question was silenced by what sounded like a gun-shot.

"You two heard, that right?" I asked, pulling my Glock 9mm out.

"Check it out," Thomas told Paul.

When Paul opened the passenger door another shot rang out, and I watched him fall to his knees before resting face first in between the sidewalk and the street. When I opened my mouth to speak I noticed a figure that seemed to have materialized out of thin air standing at the rear driver's side door.

"Open the door, Royal," he demanded.

Hearing my name had me reacting without thought, I forced two quick shots thru the door of the Range Rover. I could tell by the surprise on the man's face that I'd definitely hit him. But, it wasn't until I *really* looked at his face, that I felt my own heart stop beating in my chest. Time and a beard had aged him, but I'd seen that face once before two years ago. Suddenly, the Range Rover roared to life and Thomas had us peeling away from the chaos, forcing me to watch through the rear window in complete terror as my father collapsed onto the street.

Aryanna

Chapter 21
~Free~

The loud popping I'd heard registered as gunshots in my mind, but it wasn't until the SUV pulled off, and I saw my dad fall to the pavement, that I moved as fast as my legs would carry me towards him. The only thing running through my mind was the words *'not again'*, almost like a chanted prayer to the heavens, but I was scared, that after all, I'd done God wouldn't hear me now. I skidded to a stop by his side seconds before, Angel.

"Dad, dad are you, okay? Talk to me," I begged, already tasting the salty tears pouring into my mouth.

"Hurts," he mumbled, coughing mightily.

"Stay still dad, stop trying to move," Angel instructed, fighting not to dissolve into a puddle of tears her damn self.

"No-no time, we gotta go," he replied, breathlessly, struggling to get his legs under him.

"Let's get him into that second Range Rover," I said, pointing towards the one a few feet away from us.

By the time, we got him upright with our weight supporting him, Lil' Boy and Bone were coming out of the apartment building.

"What happened?" Bone asked quickly.

"He got shot, I think it was the driver," I replied, moving towards the Range Rover.

Bone and Lil' Boy helped load my dad into the back before Lil' Boy and Angel ran back to the Lincoln Navigator we'd arrived in. I hopped in the back seat with my dad and Bone got behind the wheel of the Range Rover. We all sped off in the same direction, trying to put space in between us and the five dead guys we'd just left behind.

"What were you thinking going up to the damn truck like that," I scolded him, pushing his shirt up to see if the shots went through his bulletproof vest.

"I saw-saw, Royal and thought my presence would be e-enough," my dad replied, still fighting to catch his breath.

"Then you should've shot the fucking driver first. You're smart enough to know that dad."

"Is he hit through the vest?" Bone asked, speeding through traffic."

"No, but he'll damn sure feel like he's been shot for a while," I replied, sitting back, shaking my head in frustration.

"I don't think he m-meant to shoot me," my dad said.

I was just about to tell him that trained bodyguards didn't typically let their guns go by accident, but then his sentence made more sense.

"Royal, shot you," I stated, flatly.

The look in my dad's eyes said it all. The balls on this kid were something else! He was crazy enough to come at us, but to actually make an enemy of Father-God was worse than strapping a bomb to your chest and pressing the detonator.

"I can't believe he shot you, especially with B.J. in the truck with him," I said, becoming more furious with each passing moment.

"B.J. wasn't in the Range Rover," my dad replied, looking at me.

"What? Where the fuck is he then, because he damn sure wasn't with the other bodyguards," Bone said, looking at us in the rearview mirror.

My heart immediately dropped to my toes because I knew the only way Royal wouldn't have B.J. by his side was if he'd already turned him over to the U.S. authorities.

"Call Madeline," I said, fighting against the bile rising in my throat.

It took some work for my dad to get his phone out and make the call, but thankfully she answered right away and vowed to look into it immediately. I knew Madeline would do whatever she could, and I trusted her, but the United States government would never have my trust under any circumstances. I'd been to the puppet show and seen their strings.

"I don't think he meant to shoot me," my dad said again, looking over at me.

My main concern right now was the location of my son, but it was evident he wanted to have this conversation.

"I'll humor you," I replied.

"He didn't recognize me until *after* he shot me.

When I walked up to the truck, I just told him to open the door. I think he panicked because he knew, I wasn't one of the people he hired. I'm telling you, he didn't realize who I was until after he'd pulled the trigger."

"Twice," I reminded him, pointing at the bullet holes in his shirt.

I could tell by the look on his face that he was completely convinced what he was saying was true, but I didn't see how that changed anything.

"What's your point, dad?" I asked.

"My point is that I could see the regret instantly, once he'd realized what he'd done. So, I think we can end this peacefully if I can just talk to him."

"Really? Please enlighten me on how you see this working, dad. What, he gives me my son back and I say no harm, no foul?" I asked, sarcastically.

"Freedom, we talked about this. He's still your brother and—"

"The day he kidnapped my son he stopped being my brother, and the day he shot me he became my fucking enemy. If you ain't realized that by now, then you must be an imposter because Father-God would have no mercy," I said coldly.

"I'm not talking to you as Father-God! I'm talking to you as just your father. Sweetheart, I understand this is an impossible situation but look at it like a parent, for a minute. How would you choose between Grace and B.J.? Do you love B.J. less because you've spent more time with, Grace, or would you still give your life for either of them, because they're *your children*?

"As a parent, I know you understand your kids are gonna make mistakes, sometimes *major* ones, but they're still your kids at the end of the day. That's the position I'm in right now, because whether I raised him or not, Royal is still my son, and you're my daughter. I'd rather die than have to choose between you two," he said honestly.

I understood the truth in his words, but I still didn't want to hear it. I'd extended my hand to Royal took him in, and made him part of the family, but that wasn't enough for his ungrateful ass.

"Dad I'm not asking you to choose between him and I. I'm simply telling you that this is *between* him and me," I replied.

"You still don't get it, huh? I'm not trying to justify, Royal's actions, but put yourself in his shoes for a minute. What if I hadn't been wearing a bulletproof vest today, and Royal would've killed me? What would you have done?"

"You know damn well what I would've done," I replied, calmly.

"Okay, so think about how Royal felt finding out that you killed, Sapphire. To us, that bitch wasn't shit, but to *him*, she was the same as I am to *you*. I'm not saying he's not wrong for what he did. I'm saying that he's a Walker and he reacted like one."

The logical approach my dad was taking was making me nauseous, but I couldn't tell if that was because I thought it was eighty percent bullshit or ninety percent truth. I could feel my husband's eyes on me through the rearview mirror, but when I looked at him I couldn't read his feelings. Either way, I was done with this conversation, so I kept my mouth shut until we got back to the safe house forty-five minutes later. I knew my father could tell I was still pissed because I hopped out of the truck without offering to help him. Was I being petty? Absolutely, but I didn't give a fuck.

"Is dad, okay?" Angel asked, walking towards me.

"He'll live, the vest did its job," I replied, without pausing in my stride.

When I got inside the cabin I went straight for the liquor supply, finding a bottle of rum to help soothe my nerves.

"Go easy on that, we've still got work to do," Bone said, from behind me.

My response was to take a few healthy gulps, then shatter the bottle against the wall in frustration. I didn't turn to face my husband, but I could feel him approaching, and I didn't fight when he wrapped his arms around me. Even though my tears were those of anger, I didn't wipe them away, but instead chose to lean against, Bone and draw strength from him. I knew, he understood what I was feeling, right now.

"It's okay, babe," he whispered into my ear.

"I *hate* that he's r-right," I said, emotionally.

My statement only made Bone squeeze me tighter, but it made me feel like my insecurities and uncertainties weren't so exposed. He held me without words and with unconditional love for the five minutes it took to pull myself together, turn around, and face him.

"What do you think?" I asked softly.

"I live and die with your decisions, baby. Always."

"I know that, but what do you *think*?" I persisted, looking him directly in the eyes.

"I think having mercy on, Royal will save you in the end."

I let what he said roll around in my mind for a moment, chewing on it. I knew what, Bone was saying pertained to how I lived my life after all this shit was over. I had to admit that, that mattered. There was no doubt that B.J. loved Royal, and as his mom, I had to put his feelings above my own. Even my feelings for revenge.

"I love you," I said, standing on my tippy toes, kissing him quickly on the lips.

"I know," he replied, smiling and squeezing my butt.

"Watch your hands, we ain't got time for all that," I said, stepping out of his arms and finding my way back into the living room.

When we walked in, I found Angel inspecting our dad's chest, while Lil' Boy was texting a mile a minute on his phone, most likely to Big Baby.

"Any word from, Madeline, yet?" I asked.

"She said there's no official or unofficial word that B.J. has been handed over to anyone in the United States. No one even knows where, Royal, is or if he's gonna turn himself in," my dad replied.

"What do you mean *if* he's gonna turn himself in?" I asked.

"Apparently, no deal is in place, and Royal's lawyers have been giving everybody the run around since that news conference they had," My dad said.

To me, that made no sense, but the idea of Royal surrendering himself had never made much sense to me either. I'd felt like we *hadn't* been underestimating him, but maybe now was the time to admit, my little brother was thinking outside the box.

"What if he had no plans to turn himself in?" I asked.

"Then why not?" Angel retorted.

"Because there was really no other way to draw us out, especially with him being on the run his damn self. He doesn't really have the time to lay and wait on us. He's definitely feeling pressure from all sides after what happened in, Jamaica," I replied.

"That seems too farfetched," Angel said.

"Which is what makes it more plausible," my dad stated, looking at me.

"It shouldn't be hard to figure out if we're on the right path," I said.

"What do you mean?" Bone asked.

"B.J. wasn't with Royal and according to Madeline he hasn't been turned over to anybody back home. So, where is he? I don't know, but I'm betting wherever he is, Royal has someone guarding him," I replied.

Angel immediately pulled out William Emerson's phone and started searching. We all waited with baited breaths, but when she looked up a few minutes later, with a shit eating grin on her face, I knew it was worth it.

"Good call, Free, a few days ago Royal hired a female security consultant from Emerson securities," Angel said.

"Where is she?" Bone asked, quickly.

"Dubai," Angel replied.

"Is she the only one out there?" I asked.

"From the looks of it, yeah, but we won't know until we're there. I think it's a safe bet that Royal, will be headed in that direction, though. So, if we're gonna move—" She let the rest of her sentence trail off, and my dad and I picked up the thread of conversation through shared silence.

When he smiled at me I knew he understood, we were finally in agreement.

"You okay to travel, dad?" I asked.

"Never felt better."

Aryanna

Chapter 22
~Destiny~

"I'm not hungry, babe," I said, ignoring the plate with the sandwich on it that Big Baby had set on the bed beside me.

My stomach *was* growling, but the laptop in front of me had my undivided attention, that was more important than hunger pains. I tried to stay focused and ignore the look Big Baby was giving me, but he snatched the laptop from me and backed out of my reach.

"Stop *playing*!" I said, frustrated.

The expression on his face didn't change, though, which forced me to give in and pick up the damn bologna sandwich and bite it.

"You happy?" I mumbled, with a mouth full of food.

He smiled his approval while gesturing for me to finish eating. Once I'd made quick work of the sandwich, he returned my laptop and allowed me to get back to work. I had every hacker we knew looking for Royal but despite there being a million cameras in London this mufucka seemed to have evaporated like mist. There'd been no updates from what was left of Royal's security detail, at least not any that left a digital footprint, but they were definitely on the move.

No doubt Royal had probably put two and two together, figuring that the family had killed, William Emerson, so he told them their entire system was compromised. That meant, I had to find another way to track his movements, and fast. Big Baby's phone going off snapped my attention to him. He immediately passed it to me after reading the latest text message. I read the message from Lil' Boy saying that the whole family was headed to Dubai, then I forwarded the hotel information he wanted to be checked, to our cyber team before passing the phone back.

Aryanna

"Tell him I'm on it," I said, using both hands to type multiple messages so we'd have everybody working on the same thing.

"Mom, Prince hit me!" Faith yelled.

"Hit him back!" I replied without thought, of course, this made Big Baby scowl at me.

"You already know that I ain't raising no punks," I said seriously.

He just shook his head as he left the room to go investigate what was really going on with the kids. I couldn't *wait* for my sisters to get their asses back, because looking after everybody's children wasn't a good look for me at all. We were family, and I loved them, but *damn*! I gave my full attention back to my laptop just as security footage was uploaded to me. When I opened the file, my heart stopped as I saw my nephew for the first time in almost two years.

I could tell by the smile on his face that he didn't understand he'd been kidnapped, but maybe that wasn't a bad thing. It would be easier to kill, Royal if B.J. had been traumatized, but based on the live feed I was watching of him playing in the pool he was, okay. I quickly forwarded the video to both Free and Bone and told them to go get my nephew. Now I just had to find, my little brother.

Chapter 23
~Father-God~
Hours Later

"Dad are you *sure* about this?" Free asked, for what felt like the ten millionth time since we'd left London.

"Freedom Walker stop questioning me. You know, like I do that in all likely hood this Seraphina chick, Royal hired knows what everybody on your team looks like, especially after, Jamaica. I'm a dead man so they'll never see me coming," I replied.

"But, Royal just *saw you*," Angel said.

"Royal doesn't know *what* he saw, but even if that's true, I don't look like any pictures that could ever be pulled up. Plus, I have a legal death certificate with my name on it. Thanks to your friends any footage of us in London is beyond even the clouds retrieval. So, there's *no way* this bitch holding my grandson on the fortieth floor will know who I am," I replied, patiently.

"But dad—"

"You two do understand that the longer I sit here on this yacht arguing with you, the more likely the chances that either Royal gets back to B.J., or just has them leave, right?" I asked, looking back and forth between, Angel and Free.

"He's right," Bone agreed, from the open doorway of my cabin suite.

"Maybe I should go with you and just wait outside," Free suggested.

"You know *damn well* your ass wouldn't be able to stay outside," I replied, trying not to laugh in her face.

I could tell, she was prepared to argue, but something about the way Bone looked at her froze the words in her throat.

Aryanna

"Your dad's, right. Besides, I'm going with him," Bone declared.

"Hold up, I didn't agree—"

"You know the longer you sit here arguing the more valuable time we're losing, right? Come on, the car is already waiting on us," Bone said, disappearing.

When I looked at Free she had a shit eating grin on her face that made me want to headbutt her, but instead, I got up and followed in the direction Bone had gone. I found him waiting for me on the dock, and we made our way to a waiting grey Maybach.

"You couldn't find anything a little less flashy?" I asked.

"We're in Dubai, a place where you come when you have unlimited money to blow, we ain't fitting in driving a Hyundai," he replied, climbing into the backseat.

I had to admit that he was right as I got into the car with him.

"You know this security chick could recognize you," I said.

"And you know that your daughters wasn't about to let you walk into this situation alone, so I'm your compromise."

"Yeah, but if you get killed, I've gotta deal with your wife, and that is *not* something I'm looking forward to," I replied, shaking my head.

"Considering that I already put up with the fallout of your death, I'd say you owe me one. Aside from the fact, that I *don't* plan on dying today if this goes right, I won't be near the action."

"Care to explain?" I asked, checking to see if our driver was eavesdropping.

"Free and I both heard what you said after what happened earlier, and as a father, I definitely felt where you were coming from. If I was in your position I would want the chance to sit down with my son. Even if it cost me my life, so I figured I'd take care of security while you and Royal have that come to Jesus."

190

"I take it, you didn't run this idea by, my daughter," I said, looking at him.

"I love my wife, but this can't be about her. Royal's pain isn't all about her, she's just been the easiest target. The only way to bring a lasting resolution to this situation is to cut the root of the problem, and your son needs *your* help to do that."

The truth in his words was profound, and it spoke to how I felt even though, I hadn't been able to put it into words like that. Royal needed guidance and love because, without either, that hate inside him would continue to grow and manifest into violence. He already had enough strikes against him as a young black man, he didn't need to add bricks to the bag of hardships he'd have to carry for the rest of his life.

"You know, we ain't never really got a chance to chop it up, man to man, but I feel your demonstration. I'm actually glad, I didn't kill you back in Chicago," I confessed.

"Thanks," he replied, dryly.

"You got a daughter now, so you'll understand what I mean the first time she brings a nigga home, I just hope for his sake he ain't got her pregnant," I said seriously.

The look he gave me told me, he was beginning to understand why it was a big deal for me not to kill him years ago, but he probably wouldn't extend that courtesy to his daughter's dude. Thankfully, that problem was some years off because we had more pressing business to handle. Pulling out my phone, I shot Destiny a text to confirm that my grandson was still enjoying himself on the rooftop pool.

"So, what are your plans after all this is over?" I asked.

"That kinda depends on you."

"How so," I replied, curiously.

"As long as I've known your daughters you've never *not* been the center of their universe, so I feel like you're the key to keeping the massive family together. Free and I already talked about changing our lifestyle, and had it not been for this situation with, Royal, we would've been well on our way to being squares."

"You and Free may be a lot of things, but squares ain't one of them. I can understand wanting a quieter life, though. I think that's what we all need," I replied, thoughtfully.

"Glad you feel that way, it'll make selling it to everyone else easier."

Destiny's text message reply switched my train of thought entirely.

"How much longer until we get to the hotel?" I asked the driver.

"About five minutes," he replied.

"Make it three," I demanded, showing Bone the message, I'd just received.

"Destiny thinks they're leaving just because the security chick left the pool in a hurry," Bone said, unconvinced.

"Destiny had been watching every move made by this bitch and my grandson since she got access to the real-time camera footage, and they never seemed to have a care in the world until now. My guess is either, Royal told her to bolt, or he's on his way back," I replied.

"I guess we'll find out, we're here."

Both of us checked our pistols before exiting the car, making sure there wasn't a noticeable bulge in our clothes before we walked through the hotel.

"They are back in the room," I said, reading from Destiny's latest text as we boarded the elevator.

Forty floors were a long way to go, but before I knew it the elevator doors were opening again, and Bone was stepping out, forcing me to follow.

"You got a plan for how we're gonna do this?" Bone asked.

"I figured you did," I replied.

When he simply stared at me, blinking real slow, I realized it was time to take charge. As I looked at the gold plaques secured to each wall leading away from the elevator, I found the hallway with room 4024 on it and headed in that direction. Once we were a few doors away, I sent Destiny a text telling her to kill the cameras, before putting my phone away, pulling my forty-four magnum out and creeping forward.

"What's the plan?" Bone asked, looking up and down the hallway.

In response, I planted my foot forcefully right beside the doorknob to room 4024 and moved inside before the sound of splitting wood stopped echoing down the hallway. B.J. was nowhere to be seen, but his bodyguard was standing completely naked next to the couch with a towel in her hand and her gun on the coffee table.

"If you go for that gun, I'll have to kill you, and that would be a waste of a damn good body. Where's B.J.?" I asked moving towards her.

"In the bathtub washing the chlorine off him. He's just a kid, don't hurt him."

"Hurt him, we're here to *rescue* him," I replied, feeling Bone step up beside.

"Rescue him from what, I was paid by his father to look after him," she said.

"That's not possible because *I'm* his father," Bone stated forcefully.

"Bullshit," she countered immediately.

"There's a lot you don't know, little girl. So, I'm gonna tell you a story while we wait on, Royal. Maybe I'll even let you live."

Aryanna

Chapter 24
~Royal~

I couldn't keep a single thought straight in my head, other than this was what it must feel like to go fucking crazy! It was obvious that my entire plan had gone to shit. But, I wasn't as fixated on that, as I was what had happened on the streets in London. At first, I'd told myself that it couldn't have been my father, because that man had died a couple years ago, allegedly by my own mother's hand. Just about the time, that I had myself convinced, I'd seen his face in my mind's eye. I'd seen the look of shock as he realized that not only had he been shot, but he'd been shot by *me*. That's what I couldn't accept more than anything else.

My father couldn't have been alive because that would mean that *I* killed him, and that would make me no better than my sisters. It might actually make me worse. I'd been battling my demons of uncertainty since fleeing earlier, the only conclusion I'd been able to draw was that I needed time and solitude to figure this shit out.

"How long will it take to get more security out here?" I asked Thomas, from the back seat of the Mercedes E class he was driving.

"By tomorrow we should have eight more men, Sir, and Seraphina and I will take shifts keeping constant watch to-night."

"Good but try to have the men here as early as possible, because I want to head to Israel immediately," I stated.

"Yes, Sir."

I didn't know how long I'd actually keep running, but I knew I had to get ghost before anybody figured out where I was. Ten minutes later, Thomas brought the car to a stop in front of the hotel.

"I'll be up as soon as I do a perimeter check," Thomas said, after opening my door and letting me out.

"That's fine," I replied, heading inside.

After today's craziness, I just needed some quality time with B.J. and maybe a few laughs with Seraphina to take my mind off everything. By the time, I got on the elevator and made it upstairs I had plans for a movie, pizza, and ice cream firmly cemented in my mind. Finding the door to my room ajar and obviously kicked in, burst that bubble of illusions real quick, and had me reaching for my pistol. Common sense dictated that I wait for Thomas, but I had to know that B.J. was unharmed. I pushed the door open slowly, leading with my gun out, expecting to find the room destroyed by whatever battle had taken place. Instead what I found was even more shocking.

"Who-who are you?" I asked weakly, wondering if I'd *actually* lost my mind.

"You know who I am."

"No, I *don't* know who you are. I know you look like someone I just shot earlier today. Someone I *thought* was dead, already. And now here you are, so I'm not even sure you're real, but I'll keep wasting bullets. Who are you?" I asked again, raising my gun until it was winking at the man sitting on the couch.

"Come sit down son, and I'll explain who I am," he replied calmly.

Part of me didn't want to breathe the same air as this man, but my legs were already moving on their own. Thankfully, they stopped just before I got within his reach.

"Where's B.J.?" I asked, looking around.

"In the other room with his father."

"I'm assuming you killed Seraphina," I said, with growing anger.

"You'd be assuming wrong because she's in there with B.J. and Bone, but we can talk about them later. There's another conversation we need to have."

"We could start with how is it that you're actually alive. I thought my mom killed you."

"She tried, but I guess the higher power had other plans. The F.B.I managed to secretly stash me away in the worst prison they could find, but I managed to survive," he replied.

"Like a cockroach," I said.

His quick smile at my insult threw me, but I didn't show it.

"Yeah, like a cockroach. The only difference is now I stand a better chance of simply staying an old man because according to the United States government, I'm already dead and gone."

"Don't be too sure about that, your daughters have a way of manipulating the truth to benefit the government," I replied, smiling without humor.

"You know why they did that, so don't act innocent. You took Free's *child* and mine. How did you really think they would respond?"

"I didn't *care*, all I cared about was B.J. and Prince being raised the right way," I replied.

"And this is the right way? Running around the world and living out of hotels?"

I didn't have an immediate response to his question, and I didn't like how his questions made me feel defensive.

"Free is not a good mom, she's a killer," I said.

"And you're not, huh? So, I'm assuming those Mercenaries buried themselves and waited to become dinner. Well played by the way. Let me ask you something, have you ever seen, Free mistreat B.J.?"

"No, I admitted reluctantly.

"And didn't she take you in?" he persisted.

"That was out of guilt because of what they did to my mom so—"

"Free don't do shit out of guilt, hell, I doubt she'd know what guilt felt like. She took you in because she loves you.

She didn't have any love for your mother, but their history didn't affect how, Free felt about you," he said.

"I don't believe that."

"Well, you can discuss it with her when you see her."

"See her? If I see her again, it'll be just like this with my gun pointed at her face," I insisted.

"How does that make you any better than her? You feel some type of way that she killed your mom, right? Well now my son, your brother, is growing up without his mother because of your actions, so should he wanna kill you when he grows up?"

"What are you talking about?" I asked slowly.

"You put them corrupt cops on Kamile and Free in Brazil and they shot her twice. She died later from complications."

"You're-you're lying," I replied, shaking my head.

"Do I look like I came here to tell you lies son? I could've easily taken B.J., killed your help and disappeared. But instead, I waited to have this conversation with you. Because you're my son no matter *what* has happened, and we're all still *family* no matter what has happened."

I could hear his words, but it was hard to see him due to my eyes filling up involuntarily. I wanted so bad to accuse him of telling me hurtful, horrible lies, but I could hear the truth in every word he spoke. I hadn't pulled the trigger, but I'd killed my brother's mom, and nothing I could do would change that.

"I-I didn't mean for that to happen," I replied, finally lowering my gun.

"I already know that, and I already forgave you for it, Royal. I would *never* raise your brother to hate you, but I know he would love you even more if you were part of his life every day."

"I don't see how that's possible," I replied softly, feeling my heartbreak again because I knew I was losing B.J., too.

When he stood up and moved towards me I started to raise my gun, but I didn't because I knew if he'd wanted to hurt me it would've happened already.

"Royal, I love you, and as long as there's someone in this world with the last name, Walker you will *never* be alone. Through the good, bad, and ugly we got your back, and that's a promise," he said, putting his hands on my shoulders.

I wanted desperately to believe him, to believe that the father I never had a chance to know actually loved me unconditionally, but it was hard to let go of the fear I felt.

"What if-what if my sisters don't feel the same way?" I asked, looking up at him.

"I wouldn't walk you into a trap and watch you die, son. I love you too much for that. Your sisters may not be big on forgiveness, but they're capable of it, and they want this to end the right way, just like I do. Come home with me son—please!"

Looking up into this stranger's face I saw myself, my brother, my nephew, my entire *bloodline*. I knew first hand that some of us were capable of being those things that go bump in the night, but we were capable of love, too, and that's what I wanted to focus on. I didn't know how to put any of what I was feeling into words, but I think my dad saw it in my eyes because he pulled me to his chest. Until that exact moment, I didn't know how badly I needed that simple gesture, but it allowed something in me to open and I began sobbing uncontrollably. I didn't feel ashamed or embarrassed, in truth I only felt one thing. I finally felt free—

Aryanna

Chapter 25
~Free~
Six Months Later

The hair on my skin from the rising sun was almost as sweet as my little boy's kiss. Almost. I can admit that the pain I used to feel watching the sunrise no longer lived inside me. I'd finally stopped having nightmares about it coming back. It was still weird to see Royal and not be looking for a weapon to take his life with, but I was actually glad our dad had got me to see shit differently. Some people needed killing and some people just needed a second chance. When it came to Royal and I we'd both given each other the second chance, because blood would always be thicker than water in this family. We were the *definition* of dysfunctional, but we were family no matter what.

"You mind if I join you?"

"No, I was actually just thinking about you," I replied, looking up at Royal.

"I'm sure those weren't good thoughts."

"Actually, they were. We've come a long way," I said, looking back out towards the beautiful sky.

"I never imagined that we would be where we are, that's for sure," he admitted.

"Are you referring to this circus that's about to get started, or you and me?"

"Both, but more so you and me. I mean I *did* shoot you," he replied, grimacing.

"True. It wasn't until you shot dad, though, that I *knew* you were suicidal for real," I said, chuckling.

"That definitely wasn't my best moment or decision."

"I bet. I'm gonna tell you something, though, and you better not *ever* repeat it, or you and me, are shooting the fade on spot," I warned, looking at him seriously.

"Okay, this sounds *real* serious," he replied, looking around before moving closer to me.

I couldn't believe what I was about to admit, but I knew it would help with the rebuilding of our relationship.

"It broke my heart to look at you as my enemy because dad raised us to have no mercy for our enemies. There were times when I thought, I hated you, but the savage in me was proud of you. I know you weren't raised as a Walker but going head to head with us showed that you're definitely made from the right cloth, and I'm glad you're my little brother," I said sincerely.

I could see the tears in his eyes, and I knew they matched mine. I pulled him into a tight hug before they could fall.

"I love you, Freedom," he mumbled into my neck.

"If you mean that, then don't call me by my full name again."

My response got the desired chuckle and allowed us to reel in our emotions. I still held him for a moment longer before stepping back to straighten his tie.

"You look so handsome in your suit," I said, smiling.

"Thanks, Seraphina picked it out."

"Royal—"

"Don't get in my business and ruin this moment we're having," he said, half-jokingly.

"I swear you're *just like,* dad!" I replied shaking my head.

"Yeah, but not even, I'm crazy enough to share a wedding day with Angel and Destiny! Whose idea was it to have a triple wedding on this yacht anyway?"

"Mine. We're Walkers, so it's always a family affair—

~The End~

Submission Guideline.

Submit the first three chapters of your completed manuscript to ldpsubmissions@gmail.com, subject line: Your book's title. The manuscript must be in a .doc file and sent as an attachment. Document should be in Times New Roman, double spaced and in size 12 font. Also, provide your synopsis and full contact information. If sending multiple submissions, they must each be in a separate email.

Have a story but no way to send it electronically? You can still submit to LDP/Ca$h Presents. Send in the first three chapters, written or typed, of your completed manuscript to:

LDP: Submissions Dept
Po Box 870494
Mesquite, Tx 75187

DO NOT send original manuscript. Must be a duplicate.

Provide your synopsis and a cover letter containing your full contact information.

Thanks for considering LDP and Ca$h Presents.

<u>Coming Soon from Lock Down Publications/Ca$h Presents</u>

BOW DOWN TO MY GANGSTA

By **Ca$h**

TORN BETWEEN TWO

By **Coffee**

BLOOD STAINS OF A SHOTTA **III**

By **Jamaica**

STEADY MOBBIN

By **Marcellus Allen**

BLOOD OF A BOSS **V**

By **Askari**

LOYAL TO THE GAME **IV**

By **T.J. & Jelissa**

A DOPEBOY'S PRAYER **II**

By **Eddie "Wolf" Lee**

IF LOVING YOU IS WRONG... **III**

LOVE ME EVEN WHEN IT HURTS

By **Jelissa**

TRUE SAVAGE **V**

By **Chris Green**

TRAPHOUSE KING **III**

By **Hood Rich**

BLAST FOR ME **III**

By **Ghost**

ADDICTIED TO THE DRAMA **III**

By **Jamila Mathis**

LIPSTICK KILLAH **III**

CRIME OF PASSION **II**

By **Mimi**

WHAT BAD BITCHES DO **III**

By **Aryanna**

THE COST OF LOYALTY **II**

By **Kweli**

SHE FELL IN LOVE WITH A REAL ONE **II**

By **Tamara Butler**

LOVE SHOULDN'T HURT **II**

By **Meesha**

CORRUPTED BY A GANGSTA **III**

By **Destiny Skai**

A GANGSTER'S CODE II

By **J-Blunt**

KING OF NEW YORK II

By **T.J. Edwards**

CUM FOR ME **IV**

By **Ca$h & Company**

<u>Available Now</u>

<u>RESTRAINING ORDER **I & II**</u>

By **CA$H & Coffee**

<u>LOVE KNOWS NO BOUNDARIES **I II & III**</u>

By **Coffee**

<u>RAISED AS A GOON I, II, III & IV</u>

<u>BRED BY THE SLUMS I, II, III</u>

<u>BLAST FOR ME I & II</u>

Aryanna

By **Ghost**

LAY IT DOWN **I & II**

LAST OF A DYING BREED

BLOOD STAINS OF A SHOTTA I & II

By **Jamaica**

LOYAL TO THE GAME

LOYAL TO THE GAME II

LOYAL TO THE GAME III

By **TJ & Jelissa**

BLOODY COMMAS I & II

SKI MASK CARTEL I II & III

KING OF NEW YORK

By **T.J. Edwards**

IF LOVING HIM IS WRONG...I & II

By **Jelissa**

WHEN THE STREETS CLAP BACK I & II III

By **Jibril Williams**

A DISTINGUISHED THUG STOLE MY HEART I II & III

LOVE SHOULDN'T HURT

By **Meesha**

A GANGSTER'S CODE

By J-Blunt

PUSH IT TO THE LIMIT

By **Bre' Hayes**

BLOOD OF A BOSS **I, II, III & IV**

By **Askari**

THE STREETS BLEED MURDER **I, II & III**

THE HEART OF A GANGSTA I II& III

By **Jerry Jackson**

CUM FOR ME

CUM FOR ME 2

CUM FOR ME 3

An **LDP Erotica Collaboration**

BRIDE OF A HUSTLA **I II & II**

THE FETTI GIRLS **I, II& III**

CORRUPTED BY A GANGSTA I & II

By **Destiny Skai**

WHEN A GOOD GIRL GOES BAD

By **Adrienne**

A GANGSTER'S REVENGE **I II III & IV**

THE BOSS MAN'S DAUGHTERS

THE BOSS MAN'S DAUGHTERS II

THE BOSSMAN'S DAUGHTERS III

THE BOSSMAN'S DAUGHTERS IV

THE BOSS MAN'S DAUGHTERS **V**

A SAVAGE LOVE **I & II**

BAE BELONGS TO ME

A HUSTLER'S DECEIT I, II

WHAT BAD BITCHES DO I, II

By **Aryanna**

A KINGPIN'S AMBITON

A KINGPIN'S AMBITION **II**

I MURDER FOR THE DOUGH

By **Ambitious**

TRUE SAVAGE

TRUE SAVAGE II

TRUE SAVAGE **III**

TRUE SAVAGE **IV**

By **Chris Green**

A DOPEBOY'S PRAYER

By **Eddie "Wolf" Lee**

THE KING CARTEL **I, II & III**

By **Frank Gresham**

THESE NIGGAS AIN'T LOYAL **I, II & III**

By **Nikki Tee**

GANGSTA SHYT **I II &III**

By **CATO**

THE ULTIMATE BETRAYAL

By **Phoenix**

BOSS'N UP **I , II & III**

By **Royal Nicole**

I LOVE YOU TO DEATH

By Destiny J

I RIDE FOR MY HITTA

I STILL RIDE FOR MY HITTA

By **Misty Holt**

LOVE & CHASIN' PAPER

By **Qay Crockett**

TO DIE IN VAIN

By **ASAD**

BROOKLYN HUSTLAZ

By **Boogsy Morina**

BROOKLYN ON LOCK I & II

By **Sonovia**

The Boss Man's Daughters 5
GANGSTA CITY

By **Teddy Duke**

A DRUG KING AND HIS DIAMOND I & II

A DOPEMAN'S RICHES

By Nicole Goosby

TRAPHOUSE KING I & II

By **Hood Rich**

LIPSTICK KILLAH **I, II**

CRIME OF PASSION

By **Mimi**

BOOKS BY LDP'S CEO, CA$H

TRUST IN NO MAN

TRUST IN NO MAN 2

TRUST IN NO MAN 3

BONDED BY BLOOD

SHORTY GOT A THUG

THUGS CRY

THUGS CRY 2

THUGS CRY 3

TRUST NO BITCH

TRUST NO BITCH 2

TRUST NO BITCH 3

TIL MY CASKET DROPS

RESTRAINING ORDER

RESTRAINING ORDER 2

IN LOVE WITH A CONVICT

Coming Soon

BONDED BY BLOOD 2

BOW DOWN TO MY GANGSTA

The Boss Man's Daughters 5